SHATTERED IN PARADISE

A DESTINATION DEATH MYSTERY

CHARLEY MARSH

TIMBERDOODLE PRESS

C H A P T E R   O N E

"Client is a twenty-six year old female in excellent health other than a history of migraines since the age of eight. No records indicating medical attention for same, nor any prescriptions for pain relief. Client uses OTC standard pain blockers. Client also has no memories of her life before going to live with her aunt and uncle after the death of her parents in a car crash when she was eight."

Edgar Bainbridge, worldwide renowned neurologist, clicked off the recorder and stared at the large black and white photo of K2 hanging on the wall opposite his desk. Although not as high as Everest, serious climbers considered K2 a more difficult climb. In his younger, cockier days, he had assumed that he could conquer any mountain—no matter the level of difficulty.

He knew better now. Failures in life were inevitable. Just ask his ex. He had loved Hillary with all the passion of a young, idealistic man, but no amount of love could prevent the implosion of their marriage. The photo of K2 served as a reminder that not all of his goals were achievable.

The photo also helped to keep him grounded and reminded him not to grow too full of himself.

Drumming his fingers on the smooth, green quartz that topped his desk, he frowned at the words on his screen. He was afraid that repairing the damage done to Harriet Monroe's brain might be one of those unachievable goals. Without a doubt, she could well turn out to be the most challenging case of his career.

His biggest fear was that in trying to repair the damage to the young woman's brain, there was a good chance that he would make matters worse. If that happened and word got out he would be ruined. No one would ever trust him again. Such was the power of messing with people's heads.

Damn Payson Douglas. His old friend *would* have to dump an impossible puzzle in his lap and expect miracles. Heaving a heavy sigh, Edgar shoved up from his chair and walked to the large tinted window that overlooked a broad canal. A white sail boat carrying a young, smiling family powered slowly down the canal, headed out to sea.

He'd like to spend the day on the water himself. No responsibilities. No worries.

Maybe it was time to retire.

"Balderdash."

He owed Payson big time. If it wasn't for Payson's encouragement and seed money decades ago, he wouldn't be the world-renowned doctor he was today. Besides, he thought he understood why Payson wanted to help Harriet Monroe. She was not only lovely to look at, she was lovely on the inside as well. She deserved a better quality of life.

Pursing his lips, Edgar considered what he knew. According to the info Payson had provided, Harriet's aunt had hired someone to intentionally wipe Harriet's early memories—an irresponsible and unethical procedure that only a handful of doctors were capable of performing.

Because of the illegality of the procedure, Harriet's aunt had kept no records that would help him track down the doctor she had used.

Still, there were only a handful of doctors capable and twisted enough to destroy a young girl's memory, and Edgar had a good idea for where to begin his search. He had attended med school with three of the five possibles and knew the other two by reputation.

Two were long dead. The remaining three had eventually been stripped of their licenses to practice medicine. Given their total disregard for the law and ethics however, he'd be willing to bet the three were still messing with people's minds without the blessing of the International Board of Medicine.

The IBM simply didn't have enough personnel to monitor every small town, village, or crowded borough where anyone could hang out a shingle and tack an MD after their name.

Edgar turned away from the view of the canal and returned to his desk. Harriet Monroe might turn out to be his K2, but he was determined to succeed–for both their sakes. He couldn't let Payson down.

Sitting at his desk again, he began to run a search on the three remaining doctors.

Miles Sutcliffe had been one of his classmates. Brilliant, charismatic, considered dashingly handsome–this last according to Edgar's ex-wife Hillary who had dated Miles for a short while. Miles had made a big splash in the media with his use of sound and aversion therapy to influence neural pathways. The media had turned on Miles when he treated a western diplomat's son and something went wrong.

Edgar pulled up several old articles on the incident. It all came back to him as he read. The diplomat's son had been a kleptomaniac. When he was caught with a bag full of jewelry stolen while the family attended a dinner party at the Swedish ambassador's residence, the father decided it was time to do something about his son. He hired Miles, and Miles turned the son into a milksop, unfit for any career path.

Despite the wrongness of employing untested remedies on people's brains, Edgar remembered being fascinated by Miles' work at the time. Edgar felt that sound therapy had great potential, but thanks to Miles the IBM shut down any further research on that particular branch of therapy.

That didn't mean that Miles had stopped pursuing it.

He put a question mark next to Miles' name and moved to the next name on his short list.

Audra Stinson had been a couple years ahead of him in grad school. She specialized in brain mapping and the use of a single electron-wide laser beam to destroy precise areas of the brain. A problem with drink had derailed a hot career after shaking hands had left a wealthy female client with stuttering speech.

Audra had disappeared after her very public humiliation.

The last name on Edgar's list was all too familiar. He pinched his nose with thumb and forefinger when he got to it. McDougall Henry–Gully to his friends–had been one of the doctors in Edgar's first group practice. Gully was a charming, handsome, dark Irishman with black hair, blue eyes, and a pronounced burr in his speech that made him seem far gentler than he actually was.

Gully had been a genius–probably still was–who employed a wide range of treatments. Hypnotism combined with electroconvulsive therapy had been two of his favorites. Unbeknownst to the rest of the practice, Gully had also been a sex addict.

At the time, he only treated women, and the reason why soon became obvious to the other members of the group practice when one of his patients turned up pregnant–impossible as she had never had relations with a man nor made use of a sperm bank.

The truth came out in a lurid news media report that almost destroyed every doctor in the group: Gully took advantage of his patients while they were under hypnosis.

The woman filed a complaint with the IBM and Edgar's group practice paid the hefty fines–and then paid Gully to quietly go away. The last Edgar had heard, Gully had moved to Amsterdam.

Edgar frowned at his short list. Any of the methods these three doctors employed could have been used on Harriet. His chances of reversing the damage would be much higher if he could study the records of exactly what had been done.

He pulled in a deep breath and let it out in a heavy sigh. One problem at a time. First he had to locate them. Neither the worldwide medical database nor a general search had turned up anything current for the three names on his list. Given how passionate they'd been about their profession, chances were good all three were operating under new aliases and keeping a low profile.

If he managed to pass the hurdle of locating the right doctor, he still had to get that person to admit to damaging a young girl's brain and then get them to share their medical records.

Payson had set him an impossible task.

One he would do his best to solve.

Which one of the three wiped Harriet's memories?

His chance of success rose dramatically if the physical damage to Harriet's brain was non-existent or minimal so he would start there.

That meant Miles Sutcliffe and Miles' use of sound and aversion therapy. If the severe headaches Harriet experienced whenever she tried to think about her parents had been induced through the use of aversion therapy, he should be able to reverse the process.

"Okay, Ed, time to track down some old mates."

He began making calls.

CHAPTER TWO

Some days Harriet Monroe felt so blessed she could hardly believe her good fortune. Today was one of those days.

She put on a burst of speed to finish her run, legs and arms pumping as hard and fast as they would move, lungs burning with the need for more oxygen to power her long, lean muscles. It felt good to push herself, to feel free of pain and healthy.

She spied Mermaid Cottage in the distance and slowed to a light jog. A small flock of pale gray and white sandpipers led her down the beach on long thin legs, chasing retreating waves as they searched for tidbits of food left behind on the hard-packed sand. The sun's rays crested over the island's central mountains, shattering the water's surface into a billion pinpoints of light. Black-headed gulls wheeled through the sky, calling to one another and anyone else who might be out enjoying the resort's fine white sand beach at that time of day.

Harriet made a mental note to bring the video camera with her to capture footage of the glorious moment for a new ad, but immediately nixed the idea. The number of resort guests who rose as early as she did to use the beach was few and she preferred to keep it that way.

It was selfish of her and she felt a moment's guilt, quickly assuaged when she remembered that the guests were free to do whatever, and go wherever, they liked. She wasn't stopping anyone from enjoying the beach at dawn, she just wasn't advertising it.

She rarely ran alone–her closest friend Solomon Ayers usually joined her–but this morning his greenhouse crew was putting together flower displays for two last minute, unplanned celebrations. Solly had already been at work for several hours by the time she had crawled out of bed and stretched for her run.

The rising sun wasted no time heating the air, kicking up an onshore breeze–a breeze that helped keep the resort at a comfortable year round temperature. Harriet pulled the energizing, salty air deep into her lungs.

Maybe she should make an ad touting the health benefits of the seaside. She had recently come across a piece explaining how sea air contained droplets of iodine and other elements that stimulated immune reactions of the skin and respiratory organs. She could even speak to the resort's doctor about putting together special packages for asthmatics and people with skin issues.

Her job as the Island Resort's public relations director was almost too easy. Every time she turned around there was another great attraction to highlight. Last week they'd made the top spot in *Pampered Magazine's* list of exclusive vacation spots.

It was easy to see why the Island Resort had ranked number one. In addition to the island's natural beauty, the resort's developer had pulled together something for every age. The wintering Angel Brothers Circus practiced new acts and welcomed feedback from the guests while they worked out the new show for the upcoming summer tour. The resort's amusement park boasted a rollercoaster designed by the famous Aldous in addition to the only remaining authentic wooden carousel in existence.

They offered five Michelin star dining, a marina with every water toy imaginable, a top notch spa, private cottages, a single hotel, miles of white sand beaches, fishing, reef diving–the list of attractions seemed endless.

Best of all, the number of guests at any one time was limited, ensuring that the resort never felt crowded. Limiting the number of guests also created an aura of exclusivity that attracted people like ants to molasses.

Harriet climbed the two steps to her cottage's lanai, stopping to hose the sand from her bare feet. It never failed to amaze her that despite a spate of murders on the island, people kept coming. If anything, the murders had kicked up the number of calls for reservations. Apparently people's fascination with untimely death overrode their sense of self-preservation.

She would never understand what drove people to do what they did.

She stepped from the lanai into the kitchen and headed for the chiller which she kept well-stocked with cold drinks and cut-up fruit. Pouring a tall glass of water, she grabbed one of the padded stools at the pink granite island and looked out the glass doors at her new world.

A pod of dolphins played in the turquoise water just off the beach. The dawn's deep blue sky would fade to a pale milky blue as the sun climbed high overhead. The sandpipers had worked their way past her cottage, racing the waves that lapped the fine sand, a sand so white it dazzled her eyes.

At that moment she felt like the luckiest woman on the

planet. The only thing missing from the moment was her boyfriend. Although at her age, the term boyfriend felt woefully inadequate and man friend didn't convey all that Alex meant to her. He had said he wanted to marry her, but he hadn't gotten around to asking her yet so she couldn't call him her fiancé.

The thought of Alex brought a smile to Harriet's face and made her heart give a little kick. When her link buzzed and she saw his name on the screen her smile widened. She answered the call and his face popped onto the screen.

"You should have come for a run with me this morning," she said in lieu of a hello. The skin around Alex's deep blue eyes crinkled with his smile. She lovingly traced the white scar running through his right eyebrow with a fingertip. With his crooked nose and scar, Alex certainly wasn't the handsomest of men, but he was without a doubt the sexiest man she had ever met.

"Sorry I missed it."

His deep, smooth voice had the power to send pleasant shivers down her back, particularly when he was whispering sweet, nonsense words against her neck. The thought made her blush. As if he could read her mind, Alex's smile widened which made her blush even more.

Harriet poured herself a glass of cold water, leaned against her pink granite counter, and regarded the face of the man she loved and couldn't wait to marry.

"About that," she said, "*why* did you have to leave in the middle of the night?"

"A domestic disturbance at the hotel got a little out of hand. The guests in the next suite complained about the noise."

"Ah. And you decided to finish the night in your own bed."

"Well, it seemed like the polite thing to do. I didn't want

to wake you. As it happened, I was called out twice so it's just as well."

"Don't be so thoughtful. Next time come home. I missed you." She watched Alex's eyes warm and knew he'd caught her point. *She* was home. He belonged with her.

"Can I treat you to lunch today to make up for it?" he asked. "I have a hankering for Chef LeBrecque's fish tacos." Someone caught Alex's attention off-video. He frowned, nodded, and turned back to her.

"Sorry, I have to go. Seems the domestics have raised their ugly heads again and are bothering others with their lack of wedded bliss. Plan on eating lunch with me. I'll call you later." He was gone before Harriet could say good-bye.

She took extra care dressing for the office, choosing a floaty, soft blue cap-sleeved dress she knew Alex especially liked on her. He had picked out the dress for her on a shopping trip to the mainland when her wardrobe had been destroyed by her stalker.

The memory of that trip and the way Alex had single-handedly changed the way she dressed–from severe, dark wool suits suited for cold Maine winters to lighter, more feminine fabrics in softer colors–filled Harriet with more warm, fuzzy feelings. She was still humming when she breezed into her office building twenty-five minutes later.

"Good morning, Jeeves. How are you this beautiful morning?"

The top of the line android who manned the office building's reception desk beamed at Harriet. Handsome in a classical-features kind of way and impeccably dressed in a white linen suit over a pale turquoise shirt, Jeeves epito-mized Harriet's image of the perfect English gentleman. Especially when he spoke in the plummy tones of an English lord.

"I'm fine, Miss Harry. And yourself?"

"Couldn't be better, Jeeves. Any messages for me this morning?"

"Miss Montgomery requests your presence in her office when you get a free minute. Shall I let you through?"

"Yes, thank you."

Harriet waited for Jeeves to unlock the door that protected the corridor leading to staff offices. Thought and care had gone into every aspect of the resort, even areas not seen by the paying guests, and the office hall was a prime example. Rectangles of light from the tall, narrow windows on Harriet's left striped the cool, cream-colored floor tiles. Brilliant scenes of the resort island painted by a renowned local artist covered the right hand walls.

The security panel to Harriet's office was cleverly hidden in a slim waterfall tumbling down the side of the island's central mountain. She placed her hand on the palm reader and keyed in her code. The door slid open without a sound and she entered her large, airy office.

As had become her habit, Harriet walked immediately to the glass doors that looked out onto a covered lanai and pulled them open, letting in the gentle sea breeze and the scent of tropical flowers. She smiled, kicked off her shoes, and walked barefoot across the pale bamboo floor to the half shelves where the cherry-framed holo of her parents sat.

"Hello, Mum. Hello, Dad. It's another beautiful day in paradise. Wish you could see it." Her parents, forever locked in a long-ago happy moment—her mother leaning back against her father, his arms wrapped securely around her—smiled back at her.

Harriet swallowed against the sudden lump lodged in her throat and reached out to gently touch her mother's face. The holo, stolen from her aunt Wendy's attic when Harriet had run away, was the only likeness she had of her parents. She picked it up and examined it closely, something she did every morning, always hoping that the holo would yield some new clue about the family she'd lost.

She hadn't even known what her parents looked like before the day she was bored and playing in her aunt's attic and found the holo tucked deep in a box of cast-off clothes. If it weren't for her father's silver blue eyes and strong chin–the same eyes and chin that she saw in the mirror every morning–and her mother's long, thick, honey-colored hair–her hair–she would have assumed the couple were distant relatives of her aunt's.

Harriet had thoroughly searched the attic after finding the holo for anything else belonging to her parents, but found nothing more. The fact that her aunt Wendy had hidden the holo and never shared it with Harriet made her keep the discovery a secret. Deep down she knew that Aunt Wendy would have taken the holo away from her and she'd never have found it again.

When Harriet had first gone to live with her aunt and uncle after the car accident that claimed her parents' lives, she had tried to question them about her parents, but her aunt and uncle refused to talk about them. They behaved as if Harriet had sprung fully formed at the age of eight and with no past.

In a way, she'd done exactly that. Her memories mostly began on the day she moved into her aunt and uncle's house. Gradually she realized there was something missing from her life. No one's memories started at age eight. She had lost not only her mother and father, but years; years only her aunt and uncle knew about and they refused to talk.

Only recently had she learned that her aunt had paid someone to wipe those memories.

Ah well, water under the bridge. Best not go there or

the migraines would start.

Harriet set down the holo. Hopefully Dr. Bainbridge would be able to help her recall her early life. Maybe she'd even be able to find old friends of her parents and ask them to share their memories. The possibility wiped away her melancholy and restored her good mood. It was time to get to work.

Harriet was deep into editing a new commercial featuring the resort's fine dining when Cass Montgomery buzzed her link.

"Cass! I completely forgot you wanted to see me," Harriet apologized. "I'll be in your office in less than a minute." She saved and shut down the project and raced out of her office to the next door down the corridor. The door to Cass's office opened before she could knock.

"Sorry. Sorry." Harriet flushed with embarrassment. "Jeeves gave me the message but I got caught up in a project and–"

"There's nothing to apologize for, Harry. I appreciate how much you love your work."

Cassandra Montgomery sat behind a large, ornately carved rosewood desk strewn with piles of papers and scribbled notes. An intelligent, older woman of ample proportions who didn't mind drawing attention to herself with brightly colored caftans and arms loaded with jangling bangles, Cass had quickly become one of Harriet's dearest friends.

One of the two vacant cottages next to Harriet's Mermaid Cottage had been meant for Cass, but Cass had opted for an employee apartment instead–citing her preference to be around people and her aversion to walking as good reasons to live in the center of the resort.

Cass's warm brown eyes suddenly lit with laughter. She pointed at Harriet's bare feet. "Forget something?"

"Oh, for crying out loud. Be right back."

Cass stopped her before she'd taken two steps toward the door. "Forget it. I only wanted to tell you that the resort's chief financial officer will be arriving this afternoon and moving into Persephone Cottage."

"Oh! I'm getting a new neighbor." Harriet wasn't as successful at hiding her dismay as she would have liked. She had grown used to only sharing her section of the beach with her friend Solly. Although part of her had always known that sooner or later other members of the resort staff would eventually move into the two vacant cottages, she couldn't help but feel a tiny spark of disappointment.

She dropped into the cushioned chair in front of Cass's desk. The resort's interior designer, Jan Rhymes, had captured the two women's vastly different personalities when designing their offices. Where Harriet's office colors were soft and muted–turquoise, peach, and pale neutrals–Cass's office was bold and bright, done in strong, tropical hues of emerald, blues, reds, and oranges.

"What can you tell me about him or her?" Harriet asked.

"Not a blasted thing. Name's Mark Fortner, and that's the extent of my knowledge."

Harriet shrugged. "It's not like we have any say in the matter. Mr. Wade must trust this Mark Fortner if he put him in charge of the resort's finances."

"Agreed. I just thought you'd appreciate a heads up. Mark will take the office next to mine and the cottage next to you so we're both personally affected. We also need to be prepared to have our expense reports thoroughly picked over."

"No problem. We'll welcome Mark with open arms." Harriet wasn't worried about her expense reports. She saved the resort a boatload of money by doing all of the filming and editing for ads herself rather than hiring an ad agency. She loved the process and she loved the resort, and she knew how to play up its assets in an appealing way that an outsider could never duplicate. The bottom line: the resort saved money and got a superior product. She had nothing to fear from Mark Fortner.

She stood and headed toward the door but stopped short and turned to look at Cass. "I haven't seen any office furniture moving in, have you?"

Cass's brown curls bounced when she shook her head. "Nope. Apparently Jan decorated Mark's office at the same time she did ours."

Harriet raised one eyebrow. "Have you seen this office? It might tell us something about our mystery man."

"I have not." Cass flashed a smile and stood. "Let's take a peek through the lanai doors, shall we?"

But the women were disappointed to discover that, unlike their own glass doors, Mark Fortner's were covered in heavy drapes.

"Well," Harriet said, pulling her cupped hands from her eyes. "What do the drapes tell you?"

"That our Mark Fortner values his privacy. Makes sense I guess since he is dealing with Mr. Wade's vast buckets of money."

Harriet grinned. "Guess we'll just have to be patient. I'm going back to work. Alex is taking me to lunch today. Maybe I can worm something about our mysterious chief financial officer out of him."

"Call me the minute you learn anything."

"Ditto."

The women parted company and Harriet returned to her office where she found a message from Alex asking her to meet him at the employee canteen at one o'clock. Soon she was once again completely immersed in her project.

CHAPTER THREE

It seemed to be a day for becoming immersed in her work and forgetting everything else.

Harriet rushed into the employee canteen and scanned the busy dining room for Alex. She spied him through the room's open wall, waiting at an outside table in the far back corner of the patio. She was only ten minutes late for lunch, but she was a person who was chronically early for every appointment or meeting. It galled her to be late for anything–especially when it was something she'd been looking forward to.

Several people called out to Harriet as she wound her way through the room to the outside tables. She smiled and waved but didn't stop.

The employee canteen saw a steady business but was never packed. It was open around the clock, with employees coming and going as their schedules dictated. All of the resort's employee accommodations provided the means to prepare their own meals if they wanted, but many chose to eat in the canteen on a regular basis. The food was always excellent; prepared by the same staff that fed the guests.

The fact that the resort's owner treated his employees on a par with the wealthy guests who frequented the resort instilled a sense of loyalty rarely found elsewhere. Harriet had never seen so many happy workers gathered in one place.

How could they not be happy? They lived on an island paradise and enjoyed a standard of living that would be far above their pay grades if they were back on the mainland.

Harriet stepped onto the patio. A tall green hedge dotted with huge, pale white and pink hibiscus blossoms surrounded the outside dining area, giving the employees privacy from guests wandering by. Sunlight dappled through the jasmine-covered pergola overhead. The light perfume of the flowers scented the air. Small iridescent insects buzzed happily among the subtly perfumed blossoms. Her sandals clicked on the patio's irregularly-shaped slate tiles as she hurried toward Alex's table.

"There you are." He slid his link into his pocket and stood. His dark blue eyes warmed in appreciation as they skimmed over her dress.

"Sorry. I lost track of time." This was the second time she'd had to apologize today. She hoped it was the last.

Alex leaned in and kissed her firmly on the lips. She loved that he had to bend his head to reach her mouth. At five foot eleven inches she usually felt like a giraffe among a herd of sheep. Alex's six-three made her feel almost dainty.

"Love the dress," he whispered before releasing her. "You look positively delicious. Good enough to nibble on from toe to ear." He pressed another kiss on the sensitive spot below her ear.

"Oh." A thousand butterflies took flight in Harriet's

belly. She pressed a hand to her body to contain them. She still couldn't believe that this incredible man loved her.

"Interesting project?" Alex pulled out the chair for her.

"What?"

A slow grin spread across his face. Alex knew exactly how he affected her and he seemed to enjoy putting her off-stride, especially when they were in public. She scowled at him—not that it did any good. His grin widened, revealing the dimple in his right cheek. That dimple had a way of making Harriet feel a little weak in the knees. She plopped into her seat before her knees betrayed her and gave out.

"You said you lost track of time. That usually means you're working on an interesting project."

"I am. I'm working up an ad featuring the resort's wonderful food. I can't believe I'm late—all the footage I was editing was making me hungry. If anything I should have been early."

"Well, let's see what we can do about the hunger, shall we? I took the liberty of ordering for both of us while I was waiting. Since you were running late I assumed you'd be anxious to get back to whatever you were working on."

"Thanks." For a man who enjoyed teasing and tormenting her as much as he did, Alex was also remarkably thoughtful. Harriet took a long drink of the freshly made lemonade he had ordered for her. It was cold and tasted bright and acidic with just a hint of sweet. Perfect.

She set down the glass with a happy sigh and studied Alex. He looked relaxed, which meant the domestic disturbance call must have been no big deal. Good.

"So. What can you tell me about the resort's new CFO, Mark Fortner?" She pointed a finger at him. "And don't say 'nothing.' I know you know *something* about him."

"Late thirties. Not married. Worked for Wade his entire

career. Here to go through the resort's financials and take some well-deserved time off, then he'll move on."

"Oh. Well. That's all right then. I thought I was getting a new neighbor."

"You are. Just not one who will be here all the time."

The waiter set a plate of cajun blackened fish tacos in front of Harriet. She thanked him and waited to attack her food until he had served Alex. The fish was perfectly cooked, moist and flaky, and the cool, sweet mango salsa played well against the heat of the cajun spice.

"I'm never going to be able to leave this job," she complained after she'd demolished one of her tacos. "The food is too good." She saw that Alex had already polished off his own lunch and was eyeing her plate.

"Don't even think about it," she warned. "I intend to eat every scrap. What else can you–" She was interrupted by angry voices on the other side of the hedge.

"Where is Okido? You've done something with her, haven't you? Did you send her away?" The woman's voice rose in pitch. "I found the two of you out and now you've done something to her. *Did you send her away? Tell me!*"

Harriet tried to peek through the foliage but it was too thick. She looked at Alex. He frowned, listening.

"What are you going on about? Don't be absurd, Allie." A man's voice, rich, deep, and melodic. Harriet knew that voice from somewhere. She tilted her head to better focus on it.

"I've never touched Okido." The man sounded genuinely disgusted. "And why on earth would you think that I'd do anything to harm my assistant? I told you last night, there's nothing–and I do mean *nothing*–going on between me and Okido. I don't know how you ever got that crazy idea in your head, but you couldn't be more wrong."

"So now I'm absurd." The argument on the other side of the hedge intensified. Alex set his napkin beside his plate and stood.

"I'll be right back," he said softly. He disappeared inside the canteen. Harriet heard his voice on the other side of the hedge a moment later.

"Miss Wynn, Mr. Haywood. What seems to be the problem?"

"Oh, for chrissakes," the male voice grumbled, "can't a couple have a discussion without somebody butting in?"

"Ordinarily, yes," Alex answered. "But you happen to be holding your *discussion* outside the employee canteen and you are disturbing the diners."

"I'm glad you're here, Mr. Hayes," the woman said. "My husband's assistant has disappeared and I'm afraid Dirk might be responsible."

Harriet was suddenly sure that this was the domestic disturbance couple from the previous night. Alex wouldn't have interrupted their discussion otherwise.

Alicia Wynn and Dirk Haywood. Two of the top names in the movie industry. A highly sought after actor, handsome, sexy Dirk Haywood usually played action-film heroes. His wife Alicia had produced several of his action films as well as a couple of romantic comedies with her husband playing the leading man. At one time they'd been lauded as the most powerful couple in Hollywood. Harriet didn't keep up with movie gossip as a general rule, but she thought she'd read that Wynn's last film–made without Dirk–had flopped badly.

And now apparently there was also personal trouble in paradise.

Too bad. She felt sorry for couples forced to live their lives in the paparazzi's limelight, unable even to share an intimate dinner out without a camera in their faces. She knew it was the price of fame, but it was one she had little stomach for. Everyone deserved the right to conduct their personal relationships in private.

Harriet realized she no longer heard voices behind the hedge. Alex returned but didn't sit. He bent and planted a quick kiss on her cheek.

"Sorry, love, but I need to go. I have to track down a missing assistant."

"At least you got to finish your lunch. Will I see you tonight?

Alex planted another kiss, this one on her lips. "Wild horses couldn't keep me away."

It wasn't until he straightened and popped the remainder of her fish taco in his mouth that she realized he'd been distracting her so he could rob her plate. She bit back a laugh and forced a scowl on her face.

"I was going to eat that," she pointed out. Alex merely grinned and walked away.

When the server returned for their empty plates Harriet ordered a bowl of mango sorbet and thought about the missing assistant. Okido was an unusual name, bringing up an image of a petite, slim, older woman with dark, almond-shaped eyes and straight black hair, most likely cut in a short bob. Curious, she looked up Okido while she ate her sorbet.

Okido looked nothing like Harriet had imagined. Of average height and build, the woman sported a bright blue mohawk, several piercings, and had laughing blue eyes that reminded Harriet of field forget-me-nots, a wildflower with small, bright blue blossoms.

She finished her sorbet and headed back to her office to work, but curiosity about the missing woman won out. Instead of reopening the ad file she'd been working on, she dug deeper into Haywood, Wynn, and Okido.

Scrolling through the news feeds was a stark lesson in how fame robbed a person of privacy; every day new stories or pieces of gossip about one of the trio popped up somewhere. There was even a photo of Alicia and Dirk taken at the resort.

Harriet frowned at the photo showing the power couple dining in the hotel's roof-top restaurant. Guest's privacy was guaranteed at the resort. It was part of the agreement every guest had to sign before boarding the private shuttle to the island. They were free to take and share video or pictures of themselves and their families, but not of any of the other guests.

She made a note to track down the source of the photos. She couldn't ask for them to be taken down; it would only draw more attention to the fact that Wynn and Haywood were on the island. But once whoever had sold the photos was located, they would be forced to leave and banned from ever stepping foot on the island again. She made another note to speak to the restaurant manager and the servers who had been on duty the previous night. They might have noticed whoever snapped the illicit photo.

Shutting down the news feed, Harriet brought up the ad she'd been working on and reviewed the short clips she had spliced together earlier. There were shots of the same rooftop restaurant, shots taken in the dinner theatre where they staged the wildly popular whodunits that involved the staff and guests, shots taken in the kitchens, and an interview with the fiery, five star head chef, Simon Lebrecque, his dark, silver-streaked hair pulled back into a ponytail.

It was good to have Chef Lebrecque back. After the chef's nephew had died in the walk-in freezer she thought he might not return to work, but he had shown up immediately after attending the funeral, as short-tempered and abrupt as ever. Fortunately it didn't matter how short-tempered the chef became–his food was worth putting up with him.

She needed more shots of food. Cajun fish tacos and maybe a platter of the one-bite appetizers chef cooked up for parties. The wood-fired pizza coming out of the oven. The incredible variety of fresh fruits and the fresh seafood delivered by local fishermen. Maybe a short clip of them coming in on their boats. She jotted down some notes and sat back in her chair, thinking.

A sharp rap on her door didn't register at first. It sounded again.

"Coming!" Harriet padded barefoot to the door. No one she knew knocked like that. She tapped the open button and waited to see who stood on the other side.

"Miss Monroe?" Eyes so dark they looked black seemed to assess and dismiss Harriet in less than a second. She stiffened and cursed herself for the way their owner immediately made her feel inferior, as if she was unworthy of his attention.

"Yes. And you are?"

"Mark Fortner. I'd like to see you in my office, please." He turned away and walked down the hall without looking back to see if she was following.

Well! Apparently Douglas Wade's chief financial officer was an arrogant bastard who expected everyone to kowtow to him. Harriet took a deep breath and let it out. She padded back to her desk, retrieved her sandals, and put them on. Smoothing her hair and the skirt of her dress which had wrinkled through the course of the day, she headed to Fortner's office, muttering under her breath all the way.

He had left the door open for her. Curiosity about what the office said about the man won out over her aggravation. Harriet knocked on the door jamb and entered without waiting for an invite.

Her first impression was that it was too dark and too formal. The office looked as if it belonged in an English manor house. A thick Oriental carpet in deep blue and cream covered the pale bamboo floor. The heavy drapes at the lanai doors–still closed–matched the blue in the rug.

A monstrous mahogany desk anchored the room, its surface pristine but for one precisely placed file. Two ladder-backed wooden chairs faced the desk. There was no art work on the dark wood-paneled walls or shelves; not a single personal effect in the room. A heavy brass banker's lamp on the desk provided the only light.

Mark Fortner watched Harriet approach from a large, deep brown leather chair behind the desk, his face partly shadowed, his dark eyes cold and assessing.

He pointed to one of the chairs in front of the desk. Feeling perverse, and also insulted that the man thought he could command her like a trained seal, Harriet took the other chair. She thought she saw something flit in his eyes but it passed too quickly to be sure. She stared at the man in front of her and waited for him to speak. He folded his hands on top of the thin brown folder set in front of him.

"Miss Monroe, as you may have heard, I am here to check over the resort's finances. I like to start by identifying the various cost areas and gaining an understanding of how they work. I'm told you are the publicity director." His voice had an unusual rasp to it, as if his vocal cords had been damaged.

"I am the publicity director, yes."

He opened the folder, slipped out the single piece of paper in it, took an old-fashioned fountain pen from the top middle drawer, and wrote something at the top of the page. "Can you tell me how many people work under you."

"Zero. I work alone."

His smooth, brown eyebrows quirked slightly as he made a short note. "What parts of the job do you sub-contract out? And please give me the contractors' names."

"None. I prefer to do it all myself." Fortner looked up from his paper then, disbelief written all over his face. It was obvious that he didn't think she was capable of doing the job. Her ex-fiancé had been the same way, always undermining her confidence. Acid began to burn in Harriet's chest.

"It's the only way to have absolute control over the quality of our ads," she said. She would not be intimidated.

"What makes you think that you're the best judge of what makes a good ad?"

Harriet pressed her lips together. She'd been in the financial officer's company less than five minutes and she already disliked him. "I know how to do my job, Mr. Fortner."

"Mmm." He changed tactics. "Tell me about this program you've dreamed up–" He checked the single page in front of him. "A program having to do with orphans."

"If you look at the numbers you'll see that the program's costs are covered by corporate sponsors. The resort had to cough up a little money for the first group, but since then donations have more than covered the costs."

Mark set down his pen. "That isn't what I asked, Miss Monroe. I want to know what the program entails. How much of the resort's resources are allocated to it? How many employee hours?"

Harriet stared at him for a long minute. The orphans were one of the highlights of her job. If the CFO decided the program needed to be cut she'd–well, she didn't know what she'd do, but she'd do something.

"The third week of every month the resort brings in a small group of orphans from different orphanages on the mainland. We give them clothing, educational supplies, shoes, and all the food they can eat while they're here."

Her voice softened. "The kids are split into groups of two or three and the resort's employees donate their free time to take the kids wherever they want to go during the week." The response of the employees to her program had been overwhelmingly positive. Everyone wanted a part in making the week the best ever for the kids. They had had no shortage of volunteers.

"The corporate sponsors get their names engraved on a special plaque that hangs in the dinner theatre. They get a tax write off and bragging rights for doing their civic duty. We take in enough money to invest in an account we've set up so every child will have a fully funded scholarship to the school of their choice once they leave the orphanage. We also look for mentors to keep track of and help the kids after they leave the island. Besides making donations, some of the guests have become involved as mentors. It's a win-win program for everyone involved."

She stopped speaking and waited. Fortner made some notes and set down his pen, aligning it to the top edge of the folder. He folded his hands again and looked at Harriet.

"I understand the dinner theatre was also your idea."

Where was he going with these questions? "Yes. Considering there are few costs involved, I believe it has more than paid for itself. The guests and wait staff love it."

Mark scratched his left cheek. Harriet saw that his nails were neatly manicured. The light picked out several small white scars on the back of the hand. She frowned at them, trying to identify their source. He saw her staring and dropped his hand.

"All right, Miss Monroe. That's enough for now. You

may see yourself out." He waited for the door to close behind Harriet before standing and walking to the lanai doors. Pulling back one of the curtains he stared out at guests scattered on the beach. Sunlight danced on the water. Kids swam with parents and played with skimboards.

Once upon a time he had loved the light. A resort like this would have been his ideal vacation spot. He pulled the curtain closed. These days the gloom and shadows suited his moods better. He returned to his desk to finish his notes on Harriet Monroe.

The publicity director was not at all what he had expected. His first sight of Harriet in her office doorway–tall, athletic, beautiful, and barefoot–had thrown him off his stride. Because of that he'd been short with her to the point of rudeness.

"Christ." He reached into the bottom left hand drawer of the desk and pulled out the bottle of Laphroaig and the short tumbler he'd placed there. Pouring out two fingers, he quickly tossed back the single malt scotch, enjoying the smooth burn as it warmed him from the inside out.

For the past year it had been the only thing that could.

CHAPTER FOUR

Alex found his second in command enjoying an iced coffee on a bench set under a palm tree. Tarbell Fox was pure Boston-Irish and proud of it. He wore his coppery hair closely cropped and his khakis neatly pressed. He'd been a good cop who got a raw deal when he killed a druggie who threatened his life and the druggie turned out to be the mayor's wife's cousin.

Tarbell's bad luck turned out to be Alex's good fortune. Originally hired as a baggage handler for the resort hotel, Fox had quickly proven that he possessed character, intelligence, and courage. Best of all, he had good instincts.

"Fox." Alex took a seat on the bench and scanned the beach in front of them. The bench was one of a dozen spread out along the path that ran parallel to the beach in front of the hotel. Several were occupied by guests relaxing, reading, and even napping. Guests sunned, swam, and walked the beach. Everyone appeared to be enjoying themselves.

"Afternoon, Alex. You manage to collar a nod last night?"

Alex cocked an eyebrow. One of Fox's endearing traits was his love of 1920's jazz slang. It was also one of his most frustrating as others didn't always understand what he was saying. Like now.

Fox grinned. "Sleep, Alex. Did you manage to get some sleep after being called out twice for that DD?"

Alex ignored the question. A shortage of sleep went hand in hand with policing, even at a swanky vacation destination like the Island Resort.

"About that domestic. The wife claims that her husband's secretary-slash-personal assistant is MIA and she's accused her husband of being responsible."

Fox's bright green eyes lit up with interest. "A missper? Great. I was just thinking that it's been too quiet around here." He caught Alex's frown and backtracked. "As long as it's not another kid missing, you know? Or another murder." He took a deep breath, let it out. It was time to shut up.

"So, where do we start, boss?"

Alex took his link from his pocket and pulled up the photo of Okido arriving at the resort. All guests were photographed upon arrival for security reasons. He showed the photo to Fox and sent it to Fox's link.

"Okido, no last name. Thirty-five years old. No immediate family that I can find. Three years working for Dirk Haywood."

"Hard to miss her with that hair. Someone will have noticed her."

"Agreed. Let's split up. We'll start with the staff, find out when she was last seen. I'll take the hotel, restaurants, and circus. You check the marina, shuttle pad, and the amusement park. Call if you find her, otherwise meet me at the office when you finish. Take one of the Hogs, they're faster."

"Awesome." Fox grinned. Other than Alex's Triumph Tiger–an antique motorcycle he had lovingly restored while still working in NYC and insisted on bringing with him–the resort's two Hogs were the only vehicles with all wheel drive and no speed governors on their engines that were available on the island. He didn't often get to drive one as they were emergency use only.

A missing person definitely qualified as an emergency.

Alex headed into the hotel. The largest and tallest building on the island, the developer had restricted its height to two stories. Oversized vases filled with tropical flowers were scattered throughout the intimate seating areas on either side of the large, central foyer. Potted mango, papaya, and small palm trees helped create a sense of privacy and directed traffic flow.

Guests tended to linger in the lobby, enjoying coffee, catching up on the daily news feeds, or simply watching the other guests. While Alex intended to quietly conduct the search for Okido to start, he would ask the guests for help if she wasn't found by nightfall.

Neither clerk on the hotel lobby desk could recall seeing Okido that day. A check with the other hotel day staff was also a bust. Alex took a list of who had been on duty the previous night and headed to the rooftop restaurant where he fared a little better. One of the day wait staff had taken sick and her replacement had worked the previous evening. He tapped the screen of Alex's link with a blunt-nailed finger and handed it back to Alex.

"Sure. She was here last night but not with her boss." He indicated a table in the far corner overlooking the jungle that grew close to the back edge of the hotel. "Dishy Dirk and his wife were having dinner at that table. This one–"he nodded at Okido's picture–"sat at the bar and had a couple drinks. I saw her snap a few pics of her boss and his wife. She left before they did."

"Did you see her speak to them?"

"Nah. I'm sure she didn't. I was on the floor all night and woulda noticed that blue hair walking across the restaurant, you know?"

Alex sat on the bar stool Okido had used and eyed the corner table. Vine-covered trees arched over the rear half of the restaurant although the limbs were kept trimmed so they didn't bother the diners. The tables were well-spaced; even on a busy night, diners wouldn't feel crowded. He had a clear view of Dirk and Alicia's table from where he sat.

He turned and gazed through the waist-high plexiglass wall that protected people from falling over the roof's edge and thought about what the waiter had said. As a general rule, movie people used professional photographers. Had Okido taken pictures without her employer's knowledge for her own personal use? Maybe she was selling them to the news feeds. He made a note on his link to check the missing woman's finances.

What if Okido had some dirt on Dirk Haywood that he wouldn't want made public? Depending on the dirt, would that be a reason for Dirk to cause his assistant to disappear?

No, that didn't feel right. He had a gut bad-guy detector that rarely failed him. Haywood felt like a genuinely okay guy. A little out of touch with the real world perhaps, but who could fault him given the rarified strata he occupied?

At the same time, Haywood was a skilled actor. He could be playing a part for Alex's benefit.

With a heavy sigh, Alex headed down to continue the search. He knocked on Okido's room door, waited, then let himself in with his master. The sitting room faced the ocean, with glass walls that slid open to the outside. Original island art adorned the pale aqua walls. Deeper aqua and cream scatter rugs anchored a couch and two chairs and a dining table. Alex moved through into the bedroom.

The king-sized bed was made, the towels in the bathroom dry and neatly folded on the rack. The small red leather cosmetic bag on the counter next to the sink looked out of place in the aqua and cream color scheme. A quick look verified that it belonged to Okido. It held a toothbrush and a few other personal items. No prescription meds of any kind. She either didn't take any or had taken them with her.

She had unpacked and placed her clothing in the low bamboo dresser next to the bed: shorts, capris, and several fitted tops, athletic wear. Undergarments.

A small red leather suitcase sat on the top shelf in the closet. Once meat became too expensive for all but the wealthy, genuine leather also became an expensive luxury that few could afford. Alex wondered if the suitcase and cosmetic bag had been gifts or if Okido had bought them for herself. He imagined being assistant to a top film star paid very, very well. Certainly well enough to afford luxuries like leather luggage.

A quick search of the suitcase revealed nothing. It was impossible to tell if anything was missing from the room.

There were no personal items in the sitting room. The small glass and bamboo dining table looked spotless. The chiller was fully stocked. He stepped onto the balcony and checked the lounge chairs' cushions; then returned to the sitting room and checked the cushions and beneath the furniture. Other than the clothing in the dresser, the room looked ready for a new guest.

Alex stopped by the front desk on his way out and asked to speak to the maid responsible for cleaning

Okido's room. He found her replenishing her cart in the laundry.

"Hilda, it's nice to see you again." The young hotel maid donated all her free time to Harriet's orphans when they were on the island and she had immediately become a favorite with the kids. Her friendly smile, laughing bright green eyes, and lilting voice were hard to resist. She was also popular with the resort staff because of her easy laugh, relaxed manner, and solid work ethic.

Hilda's white teeth flashed against her ebony skin. "Mr. Alex. So good to see you, too. What can I do for you?"

"I'm trying to locate the woman in room two-twenty. Did you clean her room this morning?"

"Two-twenty. Let me think. Yes. No–what I mean is, I checked and no need to clean. The room is spotless. I don't think Miss Okido use her room after I clean yesterday."

"Thanks, Hilda. Don't clean it again until I tell you, okay?"

"Okay."

Back in the lobby, three teenaged boys accosted Alex as he was leaving.

"Excuse me, are you Alex Hayes?"

"I am." Alex put his hand out. "And you are?" It was good policy to make nice with the guests no matter their age. He particularly enjoyed the teens; they were usually had better attitudes than their parents.

"Samuel Beckwith. These are my friends, Allen Li and Toby James."

Alex inspected the three friends. Samuel, the tallest by a good six inches, was slim of build with curly light brown hair, bright blue eyes and light mocha skin. Allen had bleached his dark hair platinum and wore it in tufts. He was the slightest and smallest of the three.

Toby grinned at Alex. His rugged body and freckled face reminded Alex of an old schoolmate.

"I heard you asking the desk clerk about a missing woman. Do you think she's dead? We'd like to help you look for her. Can you deputize us or something?"

Alex stifled a groan. Just what he needed; three eager kids spreading the word about Okido's disappearance. Still, he had to appreciate their willingness to lend a hand.

"Hasn't anyone taught you that it's rude to eavesdrop?" he asked. "First, no, I don't think she's dead. Second, thank you, but at this point we don't need help as we aren't sure the person in question is actually missing. But–" he looked each of them in the eyes–"third, if I find that she is missing I will definitely ask for your help. Go enjoy your vacation and I'll be in touch if I need you."

The boys looked crestfallen but perked up when he promised he would seek them out if he needed them. They were smiling and talking excitedly as they ran out of the lobby.

His expression grim, Alex followed them out and headed for the main guest restaurant. Despite what he told the boys, he believed Okido-with-no-last-name was truly missing. He sincerely hoped it wouldn't get to the point where he needed to set up a formal search.

* * *

"Rosie, my sweet chicken dinner, how's my most favorite baby in the whole wide world, hmmm?" Tarbell Fox lifted the dark haired baby from her playpen and nuzzled her curls and neck. Rose broke out in delighted laughter and grabbed his ear.

"Who you calling a chicken dinner?" Leonard Dixon

managed the resort's marina along with his wife, Dorinda. The couple's baby daughter often accompanied one of them to work so the other could catch up on sleep at home.

"Certainly not you, Len, since you're not a pretty young girl." Fox set Rosie back in her playpen, pulled his link, and showed Okido's picture to Leonard. "You spot her around here in the last twenty-four?"

Leonard barely glanced at the screen. "Nope." He opened a small carton of sunscreen and began loading tubes onto a shelf. The marina office stocked a variety of supplies for the guests at no extra cost.

"You didn't even look at her face."

"Don't need to. No one with blue hair has been here in at least a month."

Fox put away his link. "Fair enough. Mind if I check with the droids and dock staff in case she bypassed the office?"

"Go for it. What's she done?"

"Supposedly missing in action. Personal assistant to Dirk Haywood."

"Haywood?" Leonard paused with a tube of sunscreen halfway to the shelf. His warm brown eyes were shining with excitement when he looked at Fox.

"Dirk Haywood's on the island? That dude can act. Did you see him in *Hell Hath No Fury*? Great revenge movie. Lots of action. I hear they might make a sequel. Holy cow. Dirk Haywood. I sure hope he visits the marina. I'd love to meet him."

Fox bent to plant another kiss on the top of Rose's head. "I haven't seen a flicker in years, but I'll take your word for it. If I get the chance I'll recommend he check out the marina. I gotta scoot. I'll talk to your staff and droids and be off. Give me a jingle if you see our blue-haired missper."

The marina always reminded Fox of growing up in Boston. He and his best friend used to ride their air boards down to the waterfront with their fishing rods and set up alongside the old-timers who lined up on both side of the public pier to try their luck at catching dinner. Mostly they caught mackerel, an oily, dark-fleshed fish his mother would coat in cornmeal and fry up for him. Once he caught a striped bass and everyone had crowded around to see it. He could still taste that bass's sweet white flesh.

The resort marina's docks smelled of tar and brine and the rich, fecund scent of water. Long, hairlike strands of emerald green seaweed waved in the incoming tide. Orange starfish the size of platters crawled along the seabed and clung to pilings. Wavelets slapped the gray weathered dock boards beneath his feet and rocked the white hulls of the power and sail boats kept for the guests.

"Have you seen this woman in the last twenty-four hours?" He spoke to the mechanics and riggers and various instructors and showed Okido's photo to the specialized droids that performed a variety of functions around the marina. No one had seen a woman with a blue mohawk.

* * *

Alex's office droid snapped to attention when he returned to the security office late that afternoon. One of two office droids, both named Mary and made with identical features–short dark bob, pug nose, square face–the two Marys were an invaluable part of his team. They were programmed for combat, were incorruptible, and were one hundred percent accurate, recording every call and personal conversation.

"Anything to report, Mary?" Alex headed for the refreshment bar and grabbed a cold tube of water. The security office looked more like a hotel lobby with its gleaming wood floors, green plants, and comfortable green and blue striped chairs.

"Yes, sir. Mr. Mark Fortner stopped by at eleven hundred hours. He asked you to call him to set up a time when you can meet. Mr. Haywood called at sixteen thirty hours. He wanted to know what you are doing to locate his assistant."

Fortner. He'd clean forgotten about the CFO. While he had nothing to worry about as far as budgeting went, he hated meetings and paperwork. It was one of the (admittedly minor) reasons he'd quit his job as a New York City murder detective. The bigger reason for quitting was the general soul sickness that was eating away at him from too many years dealing with multiple, senseless murders on a daily basis.

"Thank you, Mary. I'll call Fortner from my office. Buzz me when Fox arrives, please." He unlocked the faux-wood painted heavy metal doors and entered the utilitarian hallway that led to the uglier side of security–his office, a detention room, a weapons room, and a second office that was currently empty.

Activating his office palm reader, he input his security code and entered the plainest, most impersonal room on the island. No artwork, photos, or licenses adorned the off-white office walls. The shelving next to the door held forensic manuals and US law books. A large, glossy black desk top and black leather chair dominated the small room. He'd made a concession to possible guests and placed two hard, black metal chairs in front of the desk.

Alex lowered himself into his desk chair with a tired sigh and activated his comm equipment. A quick search turned up nothing interesting on Okido's financials. As he suspected, she was very well paid. The only thing that caught his eye was the lack of any love interest in her life. That was unusual for anyone, male or female, who had reached their thirties. Barring unusual circumstances, most people had had at least one serious relationship by then.

It was time to have a more in-depth speak with Haywood and his wife. Separately this time. He was going to have to miss dinner with Harriet again. He knew she'd be understanding–she always was–but he didn't like it.

Harriet was carrying a heavy emotional load while she waited for Dr. Bainbridge to find a way to recover her memories, a load she was keeping to herself. He knew she didn't talk about it because she didn't want to worry him. Whenever he tried to get her to talk she claimed she was fine, but he saw the new tightness around her eyes and she didn't laugh as much as she once did.

Some dickhead doctor had messed with her eight-year old brain. Alex grew angry every time he thought about it, and if he felt angry, how must Harriet feel? To add insult to injury, every time she did think about her past she was hit with explosive, debilitating pain in her head. A little insurance policy planted by the dickhead in case she tried to recover her early memories.

Once the process was reversed, Alex promised himself he would find a way to spend a few minutes alone with the doctor who had screwed with the woman he intended to marry. The doctor would find out just what it meant to feel unwelcome pain.

Alex left Harriet a message that he wouldn't be able to make dinner and headed out to intercept Fox. Nightfall came fast in the tropics. He'd wait until morning to see if

Okido returned. If not, it would be time to set up an island-wide search. With any luck they'd find her tired and hungry but otherwise okay.

Given the resort's recent batting average, even he had to admit that outcome was unlikely.

CHAPTER FIVE

Clutching his leather duffle bag tightly to his side, Edgar Bainbridge fought his way through the Euro International Airport. Despite the number of security agents patrolling the concourse, thievery was rampant at the EIA. The crowds, the noise, the oppressive smell of unwashed bodies and too many heavy perfumes seemed much worse since his last trip to the continent. How long had it been?

A teen-aged female wearing bright orange air boots and a sparkling purple skinsuit bumped against him.

"Sorry, sir. My bad." She melted away into the throng with a smug smile.

Edgar patted his hip pocket. The dummy wallet he kept there when he traveled was gone. He felt a mix of anger and sadness. Anger with himself that he had known as soon as she bumped him that he was being robbed, and sadness that a young woman had no better career path than that of thief.

He didn't bother to report the theft. The dummy wallet held only blank pieces of plastic and wads of paper cut to look like bills–a plump looking prize ripe for the taking.

The bumper would have worked with a partner, one subtly dressed and unnoticeable, a thief with quick hands who would rifle pockets while the bumper occupied the target. He used to try to spot them but there were so many; over the years he'd grown tired of the game.

The taxi queue was long and loud and stank of exhaust fumes and warm tar. Edgar beat a couple in their fifties to a waiting cab and slid into the back seat. The woman glared at him and gave him the finger.

International travel was such a pleasure. Over-crowded air shuttles, crowded buses, crowded streets. He desperately missed his quiet office.

He gave the driver the address the private investigator he'd hired had given him and sat back on the sticky plastic seat. It took twenty minutes to get clear of the airport. An hour and twenty later, he paid the driver and walked into a train station and straight into bedlam.

The station had once been touted as the most beautiful on the continent. Grand stone arches soared to a single point overhead, with intricate stained glass windows set between each support. Two wide corridors exited opposite sides of the station, one east bound, one west bound. A round ticket kiosk sat dead center in the rotunda, manned with droids who wouldn't lose their tempers with frustrated travelers.

Every seat in the waiting area was filled. Travelers clutched bags on their laps, their luggage piled in front of them. Small children raced through the baggage or cried on their parents' laps. University students and their bags covered every available inch of the black marble floor.

Edgar felt a brief moment of hubris that he'd been wise enough to limit his luggage to a single carry-on. He skirted the edge of the station, picking his way over bodies and bags, and headed for the west bound terminal, grateful that he'd had the foresight to purchase the necessary tickets ahead of time.

It was another thirty minutes before his train pulled in. He waited for the disembarking passengers to empty out, then made his way to his semi-private compartment. The three other seats were already filled. He glanced at them briefly: an older white-haired man who, given the depth and number of wrinkles on his face, hadn't invested in any body or face work, a young business man in a navy suit and bright green tie already talking on his earwig, and a very pregnant woman with thick, blonde braids. The woman sat next to the window rubbing her distended abdomen with both hands. Edgar sincerely hoped she wasn't about to give birth on the train.

He set his carry-on under the remaining seat and settled in, closing his eyes to prevent any attempt at conversation. Three loud blasts of the horn sounded far ahead of his compartment. The train lurched, pressing him back in his seat, then began to move. He felt the light and dark shadows strobe on his eyelids as the train gathered speed beneath the sky-lighted roof.

It had been many years since he had last visited Prague. He loved the architecture, the cobble-stoned streets that hadn't been paved over, the spires, castles and cathedrals. It was a city that made him feel as if he had entered a fairy tale. He wasn't surprised to learn that this was where Audra Stinson had settled after destroying her career.

Eschewing yet another over-packed tram or a taxi, Edgar walked to the Charles Bridge. A young couple held hands in the middle of the stone bridge, bringing back poignant memories from his student days. He and his ex-wife Hillary had met and fallen in love in Prague. They had walked across the thousand year old bridge over the Vltava

River into the Old Town nearly every day. They had spent an entire summer exploring each other and the city.

A lifetime ago.

He shook off the memories and focused on the task at hand. Digging out the investigator's map, he walked through narrow, cobbled streets flanked by centuries-old stone and brick buildings until he stood in front of the address given to him. Centuries of wind and rain had smoothed the building's gray stone edges like a pair of soft, much loved jeans, making the arched windows, stone and metal spires, and red tile accents stand out in stark contrast.

There were several doors leading into the four-story structure. Once it had held families. Now it was filled with offices, many of them belonging to doctors. Edgar walked up the steps and checked the listings beside each bell. There was no Audra Stinson listed. He returned to the sidewalk and stared up at the red-tiled steeple rising from the center of the roof.

Of course Audra wouldn't use her real name. The investigator had told him that. Edgar had been so sure he would remember her alias that he hadn't written it down. He must be more tired than he realized. The name should have jumped out at him. He checked each door again and this time paid closer attention to the names.

Andrea Stinwell. A mixture of trepidation and excitement filled him as he rang the bell. It felt exciting to possibly be at the end of his quest. Unfortunately there was no guarantee that Audra would agree to help him.

The door buzzed and he quickly pushed it open. On his right, a stairway with an elegant wrought iron rail led to the upper floors. Several closed doors led off the hallway on the left. Edgar checked the nameplates beside each door and then made his way up the stairs. He found Audra/Andrea on the third floor. Taking a deep breath, he knocked.

The door was opened by a heavyset female with brassy blonde hair and deep red lipstick that had partially smeared on her upper lip.

"Can I help you?"

She looked nothing like the Audra Stinson he had known from grad school, but he recognized her low, raspy voice at once. He stepped past her into the bright office and turned to look at her.

"You might remember me from uni. Edgar Bainbridge. I'm trying to track down the doctor who obliterated an eight year old girl's memories twenty years ago. Could that have been you, Audra?"

CHAPTER SIX

Alex called to say he wasn't able to make it to dinner. Disappointed, Harriet decided to swing by Solly's greenhouses and see if he wanted to cook for her. Best friends and often roommates since they'd met as teenage runaways, Solly had always been the better cook. It was a gift that he loved to feed her, something she tried not to take for granted.

Solomon Ayers was a nurturer at heart. She'd never thought about it before, but maybe that was why he was so good with plants.

She followed the single lane road that ran above the beach to the seven narrow greenhouses that provided the resort not only with flowers, but also fresh fruit and vegetables. The road's pale pink crushed shells crunched pleasantly beneath her sneakers. Birds sang and called from the trees on her left. A large green and red lizard lumbered across the road in front of her.

When Douglas Wade had purchased the island for his resort, one of the first things he did was to petition the

World Wildlife Sanctuary to designate the island and the waters around it as a wildlife refuge. As a result, the plants and animals were protected in perpetuity–including the monstrous saltwater crocs that lived in the mangrove swamp situated at the island's southern tip.

For Harriet, the wildlife was one of the draws of the job. She never knew what she would see walking to and from her office or running on the beach. Other than several remote cottages on the island's northeast coast, the entire resort complex was spread along a narrow, four mile section of the western edge of the island. The remainder of the island was covered in wilderness that never saw humans.

She found Solly in the center greenhouse fussing with a new hybrid herb he was developing. "Harry! Here, try this." He pinched off a purple-green leaf from a nearby plant and handed it to her.

Harriet took the leaf and sniffed it. "Nice. Smells like licorice and basil."

She loved the greenhouses. They were peaceful worlds unto themselves–a visual feast of vibrant colors and the smell of rich, moist earth, fresh greenery, and floral perfumes. She put the leaf in her mouth and quickly spit it out.

"My mouth is on fire! Quick, give me something."

Solly picked up a half-peeled mango and sliced off a piece. "This should take care of it."

Harriet took the piece of mango, then narrowed her eyes at her friend. "You *knew* that was going to happen," she accused. "You already tried it, didn't you? That's why the mango just happened to be sitting there."

Solly just grinned and pulled the plant, shaking the dirt from its roots. "This one's a failure. I was trying to come up with a fusion of Thai basil and Thai hot chili peppers."

"Yuck. Why would you ruin good basil like that?"

"Yeah, maybe you're right. I wanted to come up with something no one else has tried. I'll have to think of something else." Solly wiped his hands on his pants, cut another slice of mango, and handed it to Harriet. "What are you doing here? I thought Alex was coming over for dinner."

"He has a missing person to track down so you're in luck. I'll let you cook me dinner to make up for burning my highly sensitive taste buds." Harriet put her arm through her friend's and tugged. "You've been here since early this morning. It's time for a glass of wine and some food."

They walked back to their cottages together, chatting easily.

"There's someone in Persephone," Solly said, as they neared the row of four cottages.

A teal and chrome resort cart sat on the parking pad in front of the cottage next to Harriet's. The silent, hydrogen-powered carts were scattered all over the resort for the use of guests and employees.

"That would be our chief financial officer, Mark Fortner. I met him earlier."

Solly veered toward the cottage.

""What are you doing?" Harriet hissed.

"Being a good neighbor and inviting him to dinner. What's wrong with you?" Solly gave Harriet a puzzled look as he knocked on Persephone's door. A plaque above their heads illustrated the cottage's namesake. Harriet inspected the beautiful robed woman sitting on a throne and holding a sheaf of grain.

"I thought Persephone was the goddess of the underworld. Shouldn't she be pictured with hellfire and Hades?" It would certainly be a more fitting image for the man inside.

"She's also the goddess of vegetation. I should have taken this cottage. It's much more apropos than a naked woman on a clamshell."

The door opened, catching Harriet mid-snort. Mark Fortner, still dressed in his dark suit and tie, ignored her and focused on Solly.

"Yes?"

Solly stuck out his hand. "I'm Solomon Ayers. I live on the other side of Harry in Venus Cottage. We were about to make some dinner. Would you like to join us?"

Mark's eyes flicked briefly to Harriet. Much to her surprise he agreed to join them.

"Great." Solly grinned. "Give me twenty to shower and get something prepped. We'll be on the lanai." He eyed Mark's suit. "Beach casual."

Harriet showered and dressed in loose khaki shorts and a pale teal blue tee, grabbed a bottle of chilled sauvignon blanc from the cooler, and walked across the strip of sand to Solly's lanai.

"Give me a hand with the salad, will you, Harry?" Harriet secretly inspected her friend while she poured them each a glass of wine and placed the remainder in the cooler. Unfortunately Solly caught her looking and pointed the whisk in his hand at her.

"Stop it. I'm fine. No lingering issues so you can stop worrying."

"Of course you are." Solly was one of the most beautiful men—inside and out—that she'd ever met. Part of his appeal was that he seemed unaware of his beauty. His sun-streaked, thick brown hair was tousled from toweling and still damp. He'd dressed in a faded tee and old, ripped khakis. That was another thing she loved about her closest friend; he never felt the need to impress anyone. He'd learned to accept and be comfortable with who he was.

"I can't believe you invited Fortner for dinner, Sol. I told you what a jerk he was to me."

"Consider it an opportunity to change his mind about you. What did you do to antagonize him, anyway? You don't often rub people the wrong way."

"I didn't *do* anything." Harriet took the salad items Solly had laid out and began chopping and slicing and assembling. "You wait. You'll see. Wait until he starts digging into the greenhouse expenditures. You'll change your tune then."

"I have nothing to hide."

"Neither do I, but he still made me feel defensive. The way he acted you'd think I spend my days coming up with ways to rip off the boss." She whirled around at a knock on the door frame. Crap. How long had Mark been standing there?

Solly rolled his eyes at her and shook his head. "Come on in, Mark. Can Harry pour you a glass of vino? We'll sit on the lanai while the fish marinates. It's simple fare, I'm afraid. It's been a long day and I wasn't expecting to cook."

Harriet saw Mark hesitate. She was surprised to see that he'd exchanged his formal suit for shorts and a polo. Maybe Solly was right and there was hope for the man after all.

"Solly loves to cook," she assured Mark. She opened the screen door for him. "He has to feed himself so he might as well feed us too." She grabbed the wine from the chiller, poured another glass, and handed the bottle and glass to Mark. "Take these. I'll just grab my glass."

Two minutes later all three were settled on the lanai. The sun was still well above the horizon and the air warm despite the soft onshore breeze. Several dark, sleek seal heads appeared close to shore in front of the cottages.

They seemed to look right at Solly's lanai before they disappeared beneath the waves.

Harriet savored the crisp melon and grapefruit flavors of the wine and tried not to stare at Mark's muscular legs. It was apparent that something horrific had happened to his left leg. Scars covered what she could see of his thigh and calf which ended in a prosthetic blade, one he hadn't been wearing earlier or she would have noticed.

Fortunately for her curiosity, Solly wasn't as polite. "Looks like you had a nasty accident. They couldn't save the foot?"

"Bomb. The ankle was too damaged to reconstruct." He nodded toward Solly's scarred left arm. "You didn't go for skin grafts?"

"Nah. Harry's always telling me I'm too pretty." Solly flexed his bicep. "I figure the scars make me look more manly."

Harriet's throat tightened. Solly had received his injury protecting her and she had almost lost him at the time. The scars were a constant reminder of her friend's sacrifice–not that she was likely to ever forget.

"So, Mark, what do you think of our resort so far?" she asked. "Have you seen much of it yet?"

"'*Our*' resort?" Mark looked at Harriet through half-hooded eyes. "I didn't realize Doug had made you a partner."

Damn the man. "I misspoke," she said stiffly, and took another sip of wine. The thought of getting through dinner with the CFO suddenly felt impossible. "You know what? I'm not as hungry as I thought." She stood and stepped off the lanai with her wine. "I'll return your glass later, Sol."

Mark watched Harriet disappear inside her cottage. He took a long swallow from his own glass and stared at the water while he waited for Solly to ask him to leave. He shouldn't have accepted the invitation; he wasn't in the mood to socialize. He also shouldn't have spoken so rudely to Harriet. It had been uncalled for.

It had been a mistake to put on shorts and join them as if he was a normal human being and this was something he did every day. The truth was, after the bombing he had pulled back from others and kept to himself. Heaving a sigh, he glanced at his host and found Solly staring at him. Crap.

"Obviously Harry has rubbed you wrong, although I can't imagine how. She gets along with everyone, has a big heart, and like the rest of us carries her share of personal burdens. You didn't need to be rude to her." Solly stood. "Come on, then. I'll take Harry's dinner over after we've eaten." He went into the kitchen, clearly expecting Mark to follow him.

Stunned that he hadn't been dismissed, Mark sat there for a long moment. He ran his fingertips over his eyebrow. Then he followed Solly into the cottage. He stood at the island and searched for something to say.

"Sorry I was rude to your friend."

"I'm not the one you need to apologize to." Solly set a fry pan to heat and pulled the marinating fish from the fridge. "Harry is hands down the best person I know. She's been my closest friend since we were teens."

Mark sat on one of the stools to watch Solly cook. "It's not her, it's me."

The fish sizzled and popped when it hit the hot pan. Soon the scents of soy sauce and ginger filled the kitchen. Solly spared a quick glance over his shoulder at Mark.

"Well, duh. That's obvious, mate. I can promise you that Harry is painfully honest. If you think she's ripping off the resort then you're wrong. She doesn't have it in her." Solly flipped the fish, waited two minutes, and slid the pieces onto two plates. Setting a plate in front of Mark, he pushed the bowl of dressed salad toward him.

"Eat. Then we'll talk."

The men dug in. Much to his surprise, Mark appreciated the simple but flavorful fare. He liked the plain white china, appreciated the crisp, cold white wine. He felt a tiny bit of the tension he'd been carrying for the last year start to ease.

"That was perfect. I'll wash up," he said, when they finished eating. The fact that Solly didn't insist that it was his cottage and he'd do clean up helped ease even more tension. People had been treating him with kid gloves for too long; he had a feeling that Solly understood what that felt like.

Maybe Wade had been right. Maybe some time at the resort was what he needed to recover his equilibrium. He hadn't always been a hard-nosed bastard. The bomb had changed him.

They settled in Solly's living room with more wine.

"Tell me about the bomb," Solly said. "When, where, why. How did you happen to be in the wrong place at the wrong time?"

Mark dropped his head against the back of the chair. He didn't like to talk about the bombing; didn't like to admit how stupid he'd been. He nodded toward Solly's scarred arm.

"Tell me about that first."

"Easy. A crazy woman tried to kill Harry. I got in the way. We both survived and the crazy woman is spending the rest of her days off-planet in a secure prison. Now you."

Mark ran a finger around the rim of his glass and

considered the worst day of his life. "I've worked for Wade my entire career. There are always those who want to steal from him or hurt him for a variety of reasons. The biggest part of my job is to protect his businesses from those people."

He took a sip of wine. Solly waited patiently. Perhaps it was that patience that made it possible for Mark to get the words out.

"There was a woman, one I intended to marry. I trusted her and I shouldn't have. She would often visit me at head-quarters. Bring me an unexpected lunch or some small thing she'd found while shopping and wanted to show me. One day–" he stopped. His chest grew tight with the memory. He sipped his wine, waited for the pressure to ease.

"One day she showed up with a gift box wrapped in fancy blue paper and tied with a big white bow." His pulse began to beat faster as he pictured that day and how pleased he'd been by the gesture. It was the first gift Miriam had given him. He'd taken it as sign that it was time to ask her to marry him.

"My office had a seating area with four leather chairs arranged around a low, stone table. Miriam set the gift on the table and led me to one of the chairs and told me to sit. She said she needed to use my private bathroom and she'd be right back. I sat and waited for her, but after a couple minutes I got up to use the comm on my desk. I was going to have my assistant book a reservation at Wade's fanciest restaurant. I already had the ring. I planned to ask Miriam for her hand that night."

"Oh, man. I do not like where this is headed."

Much to his surprise, Mark snorted a laugh. When was the last time he had felt like laughing?

"The bomb went off as I was walking to my desk. The

shrapnel caught the left side of my body. A piece of the stone table sliced through my ankle. If I'd been sitting where Miriam left me I'd have been killed instantly. As it was I lost a lot of blood and nearly died."

"And Miriam?"

"Also serving a very long sentence off-planet." The two men smiled at each other.

"And now you're back to work and here to check up on the resort."

"Pretty much. This is actually my first on-site assignment since the bomb. I've been working remotely, first from the hospital and rehab and then from home."

"It sounds to me as if the boss is trying to ease you back into life." Solly gestured around him. "What better place than a paradise island? Try to give everyone here a chance, huh? I'm not saying we're all scrupulously honest, although I think you'll find we basically are. Don't be so hard on Harry. She isn't Miriam."

They stuck to inconsequential topics after that. Mark finished his wine and headed back to Persephone. Talking to Solly about the bombing had been both easier and harder than he'd anticipated.

He stood for a long time looking out the bedroom door toward the water. A quarter moon cast a slim, silvery path upon its surface. Small waves lapped and sizzled on the beach sand. Something big bellowed from the southern tip of the island. Turning away from the water, he looked at the curtained king-sized bed that dominated the room.

Once upon a time he'd possessed a healthy appetite for the opposite sex, an appetite he'd fed regularly. After the bombing he hadn't felt the slightest desire to take a woman to bed and he had accepted the fact that he never would again.

Today Harriet Monroe had proved him wrong. His first contact with her had been a wake up call to his sleeping libido. Every time he saw her his desire grew stronger. For that reason alone he would continue to keep her at arm's length.

57

CHAPTER SEVEN

"Miss Harry, Payson Douglas is here for your lunch date."

Harriet looked at her wrist unit and groaned. "Thank you, Jeeves. Please tell him I'll be out in a few minutes." Shutting down the editing program she used for her ads, she reluctantly retrieved her sandals from under her desk and put them on.

She had avoided Payson since he had taken her to see Dr. Bainbridge on the mainland, canceling their last three standing lunch dates with admittedly flimsy excuses. When Payson had tagged her that morning to confirm lunch she hadn't had an excuse ready and he had pounced on the opportunity.

She took a minute to look out her glass doors to the beach. If she could forgive Alex for digging into her past, surely she could also forgive Payson. She knew the two men had only interfered because they cared about her. She got that—she honestly did. That didn't change the fact that they knew more about her past than she did and that irked her to no end.

Why couldn't they just fill in her missing memories for

her? Why did she have to deal with Bainbridge at all? What was so bad about her childhood that no one wanted to tell her?

That last was her deepest fear. Whatever was buried in her brain had to be devastatingly awful or the two men who cared for her would have told her, and her aunt wouldn't have had the memories of her first eight years wiped.

Because she was thinking about the past, the first dull ache of an impending headache began to throb at the base of her skull. She blanked her mind the way Bainbridge had taught her and focused on the water while she waited for the pain to subside.

A trio of laughing, tanned teen boys chased each other on the hard-packed sand near the water's edge. They looked happy and carefree.

She had never been happy and carefree. Or if she had, she couldn't remember. Would regaining her memories change that or make things worse? What if she couldn't handle the truth locked away in her brain?

The dull ache began again. Bainbridge had explained to her that the brain pain was a failsafe, put there by the creep who stole her memories. Whenever she probed her past she experienced pain. The harder she tried to remember, the greater the pain. She rubbed her scalp with both hands and shook out her hair. She couldn't delay any longer. It was time to head to meet Payson.

Harriet stopped in the lobby doorway for a moment to get a read on her friend. He stood gazing out the lobby window with his hands clasped behind his back, his posture erect as always. Impeccably dressed in white khakis and a long-sleeved, loose white tunic, his white hair tied back with a thin strip of leather, Payson was an elegant, trim, handsome man of indeterminate years. He made his home on the island and she suspected that he kept his finger on the pulse of the resort for his close friend Douglas Wade.

Payson sensed her presence and turned and smiled. Intelligent, pale blue eyes inspected her and lit with approval.

"Pretty suit," he murmured, walking forward to kiss Harriet's cheek. "It's been too long, dear girl."

That was all it took. Harriet leaned her head on Payson's chest and wrapped her arms around him. "I'm sorry. I've been avoiding you, as I'm sure you guessed. I've missed you."

The man she had come to look upon as family wrapped his arms around her and held her. "It's all right, darling. I understand. What was done to your memories was unbelievable and wrong. I don't blame you for needing to lash out. Unfortunately there aren't many available targets. I can take it, but I've missed you, too."

Harriet pushed away and gave Payson a watery smile. "You're forgiven, although I don't know why you need to be. You haven't done anything but try to help me." She wrapped her arm through his. "Let's have lunch and catch up. I want to run a few things by you."

They headed to the employee canteen and sat at the same patio corner table where she had sat with Alex the previous day. Unlike the day before, most of the patio tables were taken. Fortunately they were set well apart and afforded privacy if the diners didn't speak too loudly .

"This is becoming your table," joked the waitress as she set iced water in front of Harriet. "Do you know what you want or do you need a few minutes?"

They ordered right away and sat quietly while they waited for the food. Harriet watched bright azure butterflies flit around the jasmine blossoms. Several small peach-headed lovebirds landed nearby and searched the flowers for insects.

After several minutes Harriet realized Payson was allowing her to take the lead on the conversation. He wasn't going to make her talk about her memories or the visit with the head doctor. The knowledge helped her relax.

"Has Mr. Wade said anything to you about the orphan program?" she asked.

"Like what?"

"Has he expressed any concern about the costs—although there aren't any now that the sponsors are paying for the program—or maybe he's concerned about the employees' volunteer hours?"

"The orphan program is a resounding success, Harry. Why would Douglas have concerns?"

Harriet smoothed the pale peach napkin over the skirt of the rose-colored suit she'd put on the morning and wondered how much to say. Fortner hadn't actually said that he disapproved of the program, but he'd made her feel that he was questioning it.

"Harry? What's going on?"

"I met with Mark Fortner yesterday. He acted like everything I've been doing is . . . unjustified, I guess. I felt like he was questioning the way I do my job and I got defensive."

Payson sat back in his chair and waited for the waitress to set down their plates. He took a bite of his peppered mahi caesar salad before answering.

"Mark is just doing his job, Harry. Like you, he's very good at what he does. He's thorough and not afraid to dig. I'm sure he was just feeling you out, poking you a bit to see if anything needed closer examination. You have nothing to worry about, I can assure you. I can't speak to Mark about you. It wouldn't be right. He needs the same freedom to do his work that you enjoy."

"Oh, no. I'd never ask you to speak to him. I was–" she faltered. It had certainly felt like Fortner was doing more than "poking around," but maybe it was a mistake to complain to Payson.

"I guess I was looking for reassurance," she finished lamely. 'I've felt off balance ever since you and Alex told me that eight years of my memories had been deliberately wiped. I feel as if . . ." She searched for the right words. "I feel as if I don't know who I am anymore."

"Oh, honey." Payson's eyes were kind. "You are the sum total of all of your experiences, including the ones you don't remember. Retrieving your memories will help you understand some of the why, but they won't change who you have become–a beautiful, intelligent, generous, loving young woman. Whether you get those memories back or not, I can promise you that who you are won't change."

Tears pooled in Harriet's eyes. She dashed them away, hating that she was feeling so weepy. "Thank you for that," she whispered. She took a few minutes to get herself under control.

"You and Alex know. I don't understand why you won't tell me. How awful can it be? I keep imagining something terrible. Like I was responsible for the death of my parents, or something equally awful."

"You are not responsible for anyone's death."

"Good. That's great." Harriet gave Payson a pointed look. "Then why can't you tell me? I don't understand. Alex refuses to talk about it at all."

Frustrated, she pushed away her half-eaten lunch. "I know it's something awful. It has to be, or Aunt Wendy wouldn't have had my memories wiped."

Payson wiped his mouth, refolded his napkin and set it

beside his plate. "It's better that you remember on your own. If someone tells you, you'll be looking at it from the outside and you'll judge it from the outside. If you remember, you'll see it from the inside and you'll have a better, more complete understanding. That's all I'm going to say on the subject."

"You just confirmed that something terrible did happen."

"Like I said, intelligent."

"Payson, I need to know what it was."

Payson wouldn't budge.

"Can you at least tell me if you've heard from Dr. Bainbridge?"

"The last time I spoke with Edgar he had narrowed the search down to three possible doctors whom your aunt might have used. As I'm sure he has told you. He was in the process of locating them."

That was the last Harriet had heard as well. She'd hoped that the doctor had shared more detail with Payson, although, since the problem was with her brain she felt that Bainbridge should be reporting to her, not Payson.

"Aunt Wendy could make it a lot easier if she'd give up a name," she grumbled.

"Yes, she could. But she refuses, so this is what we have to do." Payson reached across the table and covered Harriet's hand with his own. "We won't give up until you either get your memories back or you decide to quit trying."

"Thank you, but you should know I'm still angry that you won't tell me."

Payson grinned. "I get that. And you should know that I love you like a daughter. Indulge an old man and resume our weekly lunch dates."

Harriet huffed out a laugh. "Fine. No more excuses.

Our weekly lunch is back on. You'll let me know as soon as you hear from Dr. Bainbridge again?"

"Absolutely. Now finish your lunch like a good girl."

Feeling much more relaxed after clearing the air with Payson, Harriet ate and headed back to her office. She ran into Fox headed in the opposite direction toward employee housing.

"Tarbell! Have you seen Alex today? I expected to hear from him before now. I assume your missing person is still missing?"

"Still missing. And now Miss Wynn has done a Houdini, so Alex is trying to track her down as well."

"Wait." Harriet grabbed Tarbell's arm. "What did you say? Alicia Wynn has gone missing?"

"Her husband reported her missing when she failed to show up for brunch or lunch. Alex is searching Miss Wynn's hotel room if you need to crack your jaw with him. I'm off to find her hotel maid. Plant you now and dig you later."

"English, Tarbell. Please."

"I gotta run, see you later."

Harriet changed directions and headed for the hotel. She found Alex standing in the center of the sitting room of Alicia Wynn's suite. His eyes lit up when he saw her but she could tell he was deep in detective mode. She crossed the room and planted a quick kiss on his cheek.

"I ran into Tarbell. Dirk says that Alicia is missing now? How long?"

"I don't know. Fox is checking with the maid to see if she tidied the bedroom this morning. Nothing looks out of place. Bed is made. According to Dirk, they were supposed to meet in the rooftop restaurant for brunch. When she didn't show he went looking for her."

"So Dirk reported her missing?"

"Yep. Haywood claims Alicia tagged him last night and set up a meeting for brunch this morning but then she never showed."

"They don't share a room?"

"Connecting suites. Apparently the wife likes her space." Alex pulled her in for a hug. "Sorry about being a no show last night."

Harriet tilted her head back and looked at the man she planned to marry–if he still wanted her after she regained her memories. New lines were etched around his eyes and bracketed his lovely mouth, a sure sign that he was short on sleep.

"I thought I made it clear that no matter what time it is when you knock off, you need to come home."

"It was easier to stumble upstairs and catch a few hours since I had to be out early again today."

Of course it was easier for Alex to sleep in his apartment than to walk or drive to her cottage. She needed to stop being so selfish.

"I understand. No worries." Time to change the subject. "So, still no sign of Okido either then."

"No. And now that Wynn is also missing I'm afraid we might be looking for a body. Or two."

Harriet pulled free and crossed her arms over her chest. "No, no, and *no*. We *can't* have another murder. We especially can't have a high-profile celebrity like Dirk Haywood involved in murder. The news feeds will go bug-nuts."

"Let's hope I'm wrong. I wish I could talk more but I need to get back to it."

"Searching would go faster if you had more people. I'll go change and grab Solly. Where would you like us to start?"

"You're a peach." Alex pulled Harriet back in and gave her a real kiss, one that she felt all the way to her toes. His eyes were heated when he broke it off. "There will definitely be more of that once our missing persons get rounded up."

"I look forward to it. Tell me how can Solly and I help."

"We'll start with the resort proper, spread from there if necessary. You and Solly can search the amusement park. If you finish before dark check the spa. Fox and I will take the marina, shuttle pad, and circus. We'll meet up at security when we're done, unless you find one of our missing women. Then tag me. I'll come to you."

Harriet took a cart to her cottage where she changed into khakis, a long-sleeved tee, and her running shoes. The last time they'd had to search for a missing person it had been one of her orphans. Every off-duty employee and even a number of the guests had helped them search. Because of the publicity, she knew that Alex would wait as long as possible before asking for that level of involvement.

Once word got out about the missing women someone would feed it to the always hungry news mongers and the resort would once again be in the headlines–and not in a good way.

CHAPTER EIGHT

"Solly! Alex needs our help." Harriet burst into Solly's office at the greenhouses. She stopped short when she saw her friend leaning over Mark Fortner's shoulder. Fortner sat at Solly's desk with account books laid out in front of him in a neat row. Both men looked up at Harriet.

Well, crap. She should have called and asked Solly to meet her instead of barreling in. Now she had to deal with Wade's crusty CFO.

"Alex, as in Alex Hayes, head of security?" Mark Fortner was dressed in another dark blue suit with a deep red tie and a white shirt. Gone was the relaxed dinner guest from the previous evening.

The same evening she'd overreacted and stormed off like a petulant teenager. Solly had chastised her later when he delivered her cold dinner. She flushed at the memory. "Mark's had a rough year. He carries baggage like the rest of us. Try not to be such a diva next time you see him, okay?" The diva comment had stung even though she knew he'd been right to call her on her behavior.

With Solly's words playing in her head, she made an

effort to wipe the dismay from her expression although she knew Fortner had caught it. Those dark eyes missed very little.

She forced herself to meet Mark's eyes. "Yes, Alex Hayes, the resort's security director. We have two missing women. One disappeared yesterday and one was reported missing late this morning."

Solly headed for the door. "The well-being of our guests comes before the books, Money Man."

"You're going to help search?" At Harriet's nod, Fortner pushed up from the desk. "I'm coming with you. More eyes, etcetera."

Harriet pointed to his suit. "You can't search dressed like that."

"Then stop by Persephone and I'll change. I want to help," he insisted, seeing Harriet's reluctance.

He was right. The more bodies searching–without involving the guests–the better. "Fine. I'll grab a pack and waters from Mermaid while you change."

She followed Solly out the door with Fortner close behind. Solly took a moment to lock up the office and they were on their way.

True to his word, it only took her new neighbor a few minutes to change. They piled into the resort cart with Solly behind the wheel and Mark seated in the rear. While they drove, Harriet filled them in on the missing women.

"Where does Alex want us to look?" Solly asked. Even with the pedal to the floor the carts topped out at thirty miles an hour, a precaution against inebriated guests or out of control teens. The Hogs were larger, went faster, and were designed for rough terrain, but there were only two and Alex and Fox had them.

"Alex wants us to start with the amusement park. We know it better than anyone except for the park employees.

Alex sent a copy of Alicia's photo to our links–I'll forward it to you, Mark, if you give me your number, and I'll forward Okido's photo to both of you."

They passed the main resort and veered onto the right hand fork in the road. Solly pulled into a wide, crushed shell parking lot a short half mile further along. Gay music from the carousel greeted them as they piled out of the cart and headed for the gate.

"Why the fence?" Mark asked, inspecting the tall cyclone fence that enclosed the park.

"Keeps the teens from sneaking in after hours and little ones from getting lost," Solly said. "It also keeps out any scary beasts. Harry, you and Mark take the left hand path and I'll go right. We'll meet at the water slides." Solly hurried away before Harriet could tell him he should take Mark.

They walked stiffly side by side on the winding path. Harriet was searching for a way to apologize for her behavior at dinner when high-pitched screams filled the air over their heads. Four roller coaster cars whipped by and were gone.

"Mother of Satan, what was that?"

Harriet couldn't help it; she laughed. "That was the roller coaster designed and built by the famous coaster king, Aldous. Spend enough time in the amusement park and you get used to it whipping over your head."

"No, thank you. I never could understand why people would want to scare themselves like that."

"Fortunately there are plenty of people who feel the opposite. A number of our visitors visit the resort specifically for the coaster." She realized what she'd said and felt her face heat. "Not that they're *my* visitors. I just–" she clamped her mouth shut. Why couldn't this bozo just accept that she cared about the resort and she didn't mean anything criminal when she used the possessive "our"?

"Forget it." Harriet pulled her link from her pocket and started showing the women's photos to the amusement park employees and the guests they passed. Much to her relief, Mark didn't pursue the topic. He pulled his own link and followed suit. For the next half hour they worked the north side of the amusement park, talking to everyone they met and searching the plantings along the path.

"Brax! How nice to see you." Harriet gave the mountain of a man who ran the amusement park a quick hug. Since the park was a favorite of the orphans, she spent a lot of time there and had become friends with the manager, Braxton Holliday.

"Brax, this is Mark Fortner, Douglas Wade's chief financial officer. He's here to look at each department's books, but at the moment we're looking for two women who appear to have wandered off. Have you seen either of them?" She showed him the two photos.

Braxton took her link with surprisingly gentle sausage-like fingers. "Nope. Not today." He handed back the link.

"Yesterday?"

"Day before. The blue mohawk. She wandered around here for a bit, then left."

"Was she alone?" Mark asked. It was a good question, one Harriet hadn't thought to ask.

"Far as I know. I didn't see her talking with anyone." They thanked Braxton and continued on. Solly was already waiting for them when they reached the shallow lagoon at the base of the waterslides.

"Anything?" he asked.

"Nothing. You?" Harriet slid her link back into her pocket and handed out water tubes from her pack to the two men before taking one herself. Fine mist filled the air with thousands of miniature rainbows from the natural waterfall that housed the slides. A young girl shrieked and laughed as the slide dumped her into the lagoon. Harriet knew the feeling. Her orphans loved the slides and she often accompanied them until they became brave enough to ride them alone.

"One teen saw Okido day before yesterday," Solly said. "Remembers her because he pointed out her blue mohawk to his mother and requested one for himself."

"Brax said the same thing. Apparently she came here on her own."

"Did you check up top?" Mark asked, eyeing the stepped path that ran up the side of the waterfall.

"Yeah. No luck. Where to next, Harry?"

"The spa." She turned to Mark. "Unless you'd like to take a slide and cool off?"

She couldn't believe it. His eyes were actually amused when he looked at her. One corner of his mouth curled up in a small smile. Without his usual scowl he was quite attractive.

"I'd like that, but another time perhaps, when we aren't trying to track down disappeared women."

"All right then. Off to the spa." Solly climbed behind the wheel again. Harriet took the rear seat this time. She found herself studying the back of Mark's head. His thick, sable brown hair had a slight curl and just touched the collar of his polo shirt.

How did he lose his foot? It must have been terrible, given the nasty, still raw scars on his leg. She had asked Solly if he knew, but her friend had refused to talk about it, claiming it was Mark's story to share. Harriet had been surprised and a little hurt. Solly was her closest and oldest friend; they usually shared everything.

Solly returned to the fork in the main road, turned onto

the left hand fork, and headed north again. A four foot tall, pale yellow obelisk with the word "SPA" carved into it marked the spa road. Trees crowded the narrow lane and created a thick canopy overhead. The lane ended at a plain, pale stone building set in a clearing covered in pink shells. Palm trees dotted the parking lot. Tall, furry leaved plants with gigantic, trumpet-shaped flowers in pastel shades of pink, peach, and yellow filled a center flowerbed.

"Wow. I don't think I've ever seen flowers that large," Mark said. Solly parked the cart and they climbed out.

"Brugmansia," Solly said. "Also known as Angel's Trumpets. Their scent increases after sundown so bats can find them."

"Bats?"

"They pollinate the flowers. You probably don't want to hang around here after dark."

"I'll try to remember that. Ahh. This is lovely."

They had entered the spa lobby. The far wall had been left open to the outside. Through the thinned trees Mark could see that the ground sloped away from the building down to a private cove. Small prisms dangling from the deep overhang caught the sunlight and threw subtle rainbows into the lobby. Water cascaded quietly down the stone wall to their right into a wide catch basin filled with white water lilies and colorful koi.

The tinkle of outside wind chimes blended with the soft gurgle of the water wall. A flock of small green and peach parrots called and flitted through the canopy just outside.

"You might want to book a treatment while you're here," Harriet told him. "They have everything: massages, mud baths, hot stone treatment, acupuncture. This is one cost center that I'm sure more than earns its way. It's a definite draw. Like the roller coaster, some guests book a stay at the resort just to get access to this spa. Nearly every adult guest ends up here during their visit."

"Solly! Harriet! How nice to see you."

Two receptionists dressed in turquoise skinsuits stood behind a sleek, black granite counter in the center of the lobby. The speaker, a beautiful mixed race male with mocha-colored skin, black hair, and moss green eyes smiled at them. Harriet saw that his female partner was new but equally beautiful.

"Hi, Aaron. It's nice to see you, too." Harriet walked over to the counter and reached a hand to the new receptionist. "I'm Harriet Monroe."

The woman's eyes widened. Much to Harriet's discomfort, she let out an ear-piercing squee. "Oh! I've heard *all* about you. You're the woman who keeps finding dead bodies."

Aaron cleared his throat and frowned. Oblivious, the woman grabbed Harriet's hand. "I'm Florinda Bates, Raylene's replacement. She went to work for her parents' company. This is my first week. Do you think you might find another body soon? That would be so exciting!"

"I sincerely hope not." Harriet pulled her hand back and looked at Solly. She really didn't want to let Florinda know about the missing women but it had to be done. She, however, did not want to be the one to ask. Solly got her silent message and stepped up to the counter.

"Have you seen either of these women in the last twenty-four hours?" he asked. He showed the photos to Aaron and then Florinda.

"Yes!" Florinda tapped Alicia's photo with a long, pink and white-striped fingernail. "She was in here–wait–not yesterday. No, not yesterday. The day before! Yes! I saw her the day before!" She beamed at the three of them as if she had just awarded them the lottery. "Do you think she's dead?"

"Thank you, Florinda," Solly said. He turned to Harriet and Mark. "Let's go."

"So, that was a bust," Mark said, once they were outside and out of earshot.

"The thought of a dead guest didn't seem to faze Florinda at all. Quite the opposite in fact–she looked excited by the prospect." Harriet shook her head. "Poor Aaron." Mark's dark eyebrows furrowed. "What?"

"You keep finding dead bodies?"

"No. Well, maybe one or two." She turned away before he could press her for more information.

"We'll search outside, check the grounds down to the cove and around the parking lot before we leave," Solly told them. "I have a feeling our new employee is going to tell all her friends about meeting Harriet and that we're looking for two women. It won't take long for the news feeds to discover Alicia Wynn is missing."

They split up and searched the grounds but turned up nothing. Harriet handed out more water and called Alex to see if he wanted them to look anywhere else before they headed back to the main resort and the security office.

"Tarbell and Alex haven't come up with anything either," she said, ending the call. "Alex asked if we had time to search the pirate coves since we're closest."

"Absolutely." Solly turned left when they hit the main road.

"Pirate coves?" Mark raised one eyebrow, looked skeptical. "Were there real pirates on this island?"

"You bet," Harriet answered from the back seat. "There was even buried treasure, although the treasure has been found. Or at least one has. For all I know there could be more. I don't think anyone knows for sure which pirates visited here, but the resort cottage coves are named for the four likeliest: Kidd, Morgan, Black Bart, and Blackbeard. Black Bart's cove has a partially sunken shipwreck that's popular with the divers."

Solly waited for a large green and red parrot to grab a fallen fruit from the road and fly off with its prize before turning down a lane marked Morgan's Cove. The trees soon gave way to a wide cove with a C-shaped white sand beach and a half dozen well-spaced, single story cottages. A family with four children played in the water in front of the largest cottage.

"Every cottage in the pirate coves sits near the water," Harriet told Mark. "The largest have four bedrooms; the smallest have two, slightly larger than ours. Morgan's Cove is great for families with young children because the water is shallow for quite a ways out." A soft breeze ruffled the turquoise water and carried the scent of coconut sunscreen to them.

Why didn't Mark know more of the details of the resort? As chief financial officer for Wade Industries she would have thought that he'd be on top of all Wade projects, especially one as important to Wade as the resort was. It made no sense.

"How do you want to do this?" asked Solly, breaking into Harriet's thoughts. "Shall we knock on doors and then search around each cottage?"

"I'll start at the far end," Mark said, as he climbed out of the jeep. He headed for the farthest cottage before anyone could suggest otherwise.

"Solly." Harriet grabbed her friend's arm. "What's with that guy? What's he trying to prove?" Her link buzzed in her pocket before Solly could answer.

"Wait a minute, Mark!" she called. "It's Alex!" Her hands

were shaking when she dropped the link back in her pocket.

"Bad news. Leonard just called Alex from the marina. Some teens found Alicia Wynn's body trapped underneath one of the docks."

It took them fifteen minutes to drive to the marina.

"I could run faster than this thing moves," Mark complained. "Can't you go any faster, Solly?"

"Nope. This is top speed."

"I'd like to see you run faster," Harriet said from the back seat. "A human can barely top twenty-three miles an hour and that's for a very short period. The carts do thirty until they run out of fuel."

"Well, aren't you full of trivial information." Mark scowled over his shoulder at her. "And I do mean trivial."

"When I first came to the resort these carts drove me nuts." Solly broke in before Harriet could pursue the argument. "I was sure I could get where I was going faster if I ran, so I looked it up. Harry's right. The fastest sprinter in the world can't quite hit twenty-four miles an hour and that's a short sprint. Imagine keeping that up for miles."

He turned into the marina parking lot, parked, and grinned at Mark. "Spend a few months here and you'll realize that the carts go fast enough. One of the major appeals of island life is the slower pace."

"Not for me, mate. I don't like to waste time."

Inwardly, Harriet scoffed at Mark's attitude. He was a typical type A—a driven bureaucrat bulling his way through life. Surly and unpleasant when things didn't go his way. Get things done, move on to the next thing without ever taking time to appreciate the beauty in the world. Not the kind of person she wanted in her life. Fortunately he was only there on temporary assignment.

CHAPTER NINE

The marina was at a standstill. Usually one of the busiest attractions of the resort, it was strange not to see guests out on the water.

Harriet climbed out of the cart and moved to stand next to Solly, keeping him between her and Mark.

Both of the security office Hogs were parked near the docks. Workers and droids stood in the parking lot in small groups. The workers talked quietly, the droids stood silent and still, waiting for instructions. Three teen boys stood huddled close together. She recognized them as the same trio she'd seen racing each other on the beach. They had been laughing and shouting then, now they looked shaken. The tallest of the three spun suddenly and vomited.

Harriet spied the spa's doctor kneeling beside a body laid out on the dock that housed the sailboats. Tarbell and Leonard stood behind her. Harriet searched for Alex and found him kneeling at the edge of the dock looking at something in the water.

"We shouldn't go down there," Solly said. "I'm sure any

evidence has been destroyed already but we don't want to add to the issue."

Alex stood then and spied them. He spoke to Leonard and both men headed toward the parking lot. Leonard's face looked sickly pale as he passed them and went into the marina office. Alex stopped to speak to the teens. They nodded at whatever he said and left in a resort cart.

"Is Leonard going to be all right?" Harriet asked Alex when he joined them.

"Eventually. It's not pretty. Miss Wynn was covered in crabs when we pulled her out. What are you doing here?"

"We came to see if there was anything we could do to help. Do you know how she died?"

"Difficult to say at the moment. Eleanor estimates she went into the water sometime last night. Miss Wynn sustained a skull injury but that could have happened in the water or before. Eleanor will fly the body to the lab on the mainland and do an autopsy, let us know."

The body. Harriet shuddered, thankful that she hadn't been the one to find Alicia Wynn. "Is there anything we can do to help?"

"Not here, but we still need to locate Okido. Unless you've heard something different, no one has seen her since the day before yesterday. Our last confirmed sighting is Monday evening at the roof-top restaurant."

"Oh!" Harriet laid her hand on Alex's arm. "I saw a photo of Alicia and Dirk taken in the restaurant in the tabloids. I was going to try to track down the photographer. Do you think it might have been Okido?"

"I know it was. One of the waitstaff said she sat at the bar, didn't approach Alicia or Dirk, and he saw her snap a few shots of her employer and his wife."

"Why would she do that?" Solly asked. "Doesn't she

have access to them all the time? And why sell the pics to the paparazzi? That could cost her her job."

"You're asking me? These people are way out of my league. Now that we've found Miss Wynn I'm afraid we'll have to make Okido's disappearance public and ask anyone who saw or spoke with her to tag me or Fox. Hopefully we'll find her alive," he added, his expression grim.

He leaned in for a kiss and brushed Harriet's lips lightly with his own. "I need to get back to Fox and Eleanor. I'll most likely sleep at my apartment tonight."

Harriet frowned but didn't argue. She knew that Alex would work around the clock now that he had a body. "What does your gut tell you, Alex?" she asked. "Murder or accident? And please say accident."

Alex's expression was grim. "It's too soon to say, but I don't think you're going to like the answer."

"That's what I was afraid of." Harriet heaved a sigh. "Okay. We'll keep looking for Okido."

"Thanks. Fox and I have already checked with the circus people. We were headed for the pirate coves when Leonard called. Other than the waiter at the restaurant, so far no one reports sighting either woman." He turned and headed back toward the docks.

"I want to check on Leonard before we take off," Harriet said. She headed toward the marina office with Solly and Mark on her heels.

They found Leonard leaning against the counter with baby Rose in his arms. "I needed a reminder of what is good and beautiful in the world," he said, bending his neck to plant a kiss on Rose's neck. His daughter grabbed his ear and giggled.

"Leonard, have you met Mark Fortner? He's the CFO for Wade Industries. We're helping Alex search for Dirk Haywood's personal assistant, Okido." Harriet turned to

Mark. "This is Leonard Dixon. He and his wife Dorinda manage the marina." The men nodded at one another.

"Alex asked me about Okido yesterday. I haven't seen her. I checked with Dorie and she hasn't either."

"Would you like me to call Dorie and ask her to come in so you can leave?"

"Thanks, Harry, but no. I already called her. Dorie's on her way. I need to have my family with me. I need to know they're safe." His warm brown eyes, eyes that were generally filled with laughter, looked haunted. "I'll never forget the sight of that poor woman when they pulled her from the water. Crabs, for chrissakes." He shook his head.

The bell over the door jangled and a petite woman with dark curls ran in and straight to Leonard.

"Dorie." Leonard spread one arm and pulled his wife into a hug.

Harriet felt a tug of jealousy. She wanted a family, wanted that closeness that Leonard and Dorinda shared. She knew it had to wait until the mess in her brain was sorted, but creating a family was high on her list of dreams. She led the way out of the office to give the Dixons privacy.

They were quiet as they piled back into the cart. This time Mark took the wheel and Solly sat in the back before Harriet could grab the seat, forcing her to sit next to Mark. She glared at Solly and he responded with raised eyebrows and a smirk.

"Where to first?" Mark asked. "You two know the island. Where should we look for someone who's been missing for two days?"

"All the obvious places have been searched. I think we need to know more about Okido. It might help us know where to look," Harriet said. "Let's track down Dirk Haywood and see what he can tell us about her."

"If we all go he'll feel like we're ganging up on him," Solly pointed out. "I think two of us should talk to Dirk. I'm going."

"I'm going," Harriet said.

"I'm going," Mark said. They glared at one another. Much to Harriet's amazement, Mark laughed. A dimple appeared in his right cheek and his dark eyes sparkled with humor. She hated to admit it, but the man's smiles were growing on her.

"It looks like we're all going to talk with Mr. Haywood," Mark said. "He can take it–he's a big tough action hero after all." He started the cart and exited the marina parking lot, still smiling. Harriet didn't speak at all on the way back to the hotel. She wasn't sure what to make of a Mark Fortner who behaved like a normal human being.

They found Dirk down by the water, arms crossed over his chest, staring at the horizon. The three boys who had discovered his wife's body stood a ways off, giving him curious looks and nudging each other. Several black-headed gulls bobbed on the water in front of the actor, hopeful for a handout.

Harriet didn't think that Dirk was aware of any of it. She touched him lightly on the shoulder.

"Mr. Haywood?" She took a step back from the anger in his eyes when he looked at her.

"What do you want? I'm not signing any damn auto-graphs. And if you want to know how I feel about my wife being murdered, I'm devastated. Now leave me alone."

Mark joined Harriet. "Mr. Haywood. We aren't inter-ested in autographs. We work for the resort." He held out a hand. "I'm Mark Fortner, the chief financial officer. This is Harriet Monroe, the director of public relations, and Solomon Ayers, the head green thumb."

Dirk huffed an exasperated sigh but reached out a

reluctant hand and gave Mark's a quick shake. "Fine. What do you want?"

"We just came from the marina," Harriet said. "I'm very sorry for your loss."

"I was told to stay near the hotel until I heard from Hayes. Why did he let you see my wife when I can't? It's not right. It's not right. I need to see my wife."

"We didn't see Alicia," Solly said quickly. "Alex asked us to keep looking for Okido and we were wondering if you could tell us anything about her that might help us find her. How did she come to work for you?"

The teens had crept closer and were listening. Dirk scowled at them. "Let's walk." He led the way down the beach with Harriet and the others tagging along. Once they were well away from any eavesdroppers Dirk stopped.

"Don't ever become a film star. You lose all right to any privacy."

"I don't think I have to worry about that," Solly said. "I value my privacy too much. Can you tell us how Okido came to work for you? Did you hire her through an agency of some sort?"

"Nah. I knew her from a couple of my films. Okido was a stunt double for two of my co-stars. A good one too, always busy with work–until she lost her nerve. No matter how much prep work and precautions are taken, there's always a risk of injury. One of the stuntmen on the second film we worked together on crashed into a wall and was paralyzed from the waist down. Okido quit the next day."

"That's awful." No amount of insurance a stunt double had to carry could make up for a life suddenly relegated to a wheelchair. Harriet didn't blame Okido for making a career change.

Dirk shrugged. "It's hazardous work. Injuries happen fairly often. Fortunately most are minor."

"So Okido went to work for you after she quit?" Mark asked.

"No. The assistant I'd had from my first movie on retired three years ago to look after her grandchildren. Marta was great. She'd been around film people all of her life and she wasn't impressed or intimidated by the movie crowd. I couldn't have asked for a better assistant. She taught me the ropes, how to get along with big egos, who to trust and who to avoid. I hated losing her.

"When Marta left, my wife hired Okido before I could do a proper search for a replacement. I was busy then with back-to-back films so I took Okido on a trial basis. Then I stayed busy and didn't have time to replace her." He shrugged. "Maybe that isn't quite fair. Marta set the bar impossibly high. Okido isn't Marta, but she does an okay job."

"Mr. Haywood, were you and Okido having an affair?"

Harriet gave Mark a warning look. That was the kind of question Alex should ask.

The actor looked insulted. "Lord, no. I find nothing attractive about Okido. I prefer my women to be softer, more feminine." His voice tightened and his eyes grew shiny with unshed tears. "I loved my wife." After a few moments he cleared his throat. "To be honest I'm not even sure Okido likes men."

"What makes you say that?" Harriet asked. She hoped Dirk Haywood wasn't one of those men who accused a woman of being a lesbian when she showed no interest in him.

"In all the time I've known her I've never seen her with a man. When she goes out she favors female companions."

"Does Okido have any enemies that you're aware of?" Solly asked. "Or suicidal tendencies?"

Dirk shook his head. "Not that I'm aware of to both those questions." He stared out at the water. "We'd been arguing a lot lately."

"You and Okido?" Solly asked.

"No, me and Alicia. I don't even know why. It was as if Allie was looking for things to fight about. Then she sprang this trip on me. I didn't even want to come to this damn island but she thought it would be good for us to get away, go somewhere where the news mongers couldn't find us, so I agreed. When she asked Okido to come along we had an argument about that. Why would I want to bring my damn assistant with me on vacation?"

"Was that why Alex was called to the hotel? You were arguing?" Harriet asked. She wondered how he felt, knowing that his last days with his wife were spent arguing. She would have a hard time dealing if she was in his place.

"Yeah." Dirk looked at her, his eyes still shiny. "We worked it out, that night she disappeared. We worked it out. I was going to send Okido home so we could have the remainder of the week to ourselves." He turned back to the water but kept speaking, his voice low.

"We were going to push off a few projects and pace ourselves better so we'd have more time together. That was the problem, you see. Our work had taken over our lives and we lost touch with why we got married in the first place."

No one said anything for several minutes. Finally Dirk turned to them. "Are we done here? I need to speak with Alex Hayes. I need to make arrangements for my wife and figure out what to do next."

"Thank you for your time, Mr. Haywood," Harriet said.

She touched him lightly on the arm. "I'm truly sorry for your loss. Alicia Wynn was an important advocate for women in the film industry. Her death is a loss for everyone."

Dirk Haywood turned back in the direction of the hotel and headed up the beach at a slow jog.

"Did we get anything useful from that?" Mark asked, once the actor was out of earshot.

"Two things," Harriet said. "One, Okido was a stunt double."

Solly pointed at Harriet. "That means she has moves and tricks. She's not a helpless maiden."

"Exactly. And two, it's possible that she preferred women to men. What if there was something going on between her and Alicia Wynn and that was the reason for the arguments?"

"So you're saying that Okido and Alicia were having an affair? I can't imagine a man like Dirk Haywood would care for that." Mark looked intrigued. "Interesting. But how does that help us find her?"

"I don't know if it does. I'm just tossing out thoughts. I'm also thirsty and our waters are gone. Our cottages aren't far from here. Let's get something to drink and regroup, take a few minutes to come up with a search plan."

Ten minutes later they sat in Harriet's living room with cold waters, Harriet and Mark in the two chairs and Solly sprawled on the couch. The doors were open to the lanai and the ocean breeze. The mahogany paneled walls and ceiling were a welcome respite from the bright tropical sun.

"What if Harry's onto something and Dirk Haywood found out that his wife and personal assistant were having an affair?" Solly said. "That could be potentially devastating to the reputation of a macho, action-hero film star."

"It could be even more devastating to a handsome romantic lead," Harriet pointed out. "So are you saying Dirk killed Alicia and Okido?"

Solly shrugged one shoulder. "It's possible. Unappealing, but possible. Who wants one of the world's best known heroes to be sent up for a double homicide? Not me. I love the guy."

"That's not something we can solve," Mark said. "Our job is to look for Okido."

"I vote for a methodical search of the resort, starting at the southern tip of the island." Harriet stood. "This time I get to drive." She saw Mark cut his eyes toward her. "You have a problem with that, Mr. Fortner?" she asked sweetly.

"Say no, Mark. It's not worth arguing. Harry will win and you'll just end up either confused or frustrated." Solly stood and walked into the kitchen. "I'll grab more waters," he called out. "We ready to go?"

There was nothing on the southern tip of the island for the guests other than the mangrove swamp. The pristine beach was usually deserted except for the serious runners and walkers. Harriet drove past several low stone buildings that housed necessary functions for the resort. The laundry sat next to a long garage that provided extra storage and serviced the water toys for the marina. Behind them stood Solly's seven greenhouses.

Once they passed the last of the resort buildings there was no sign of civilization to be seen. Ocean lapped the white sand on their right, with only a faint smudge on the horizon to indicate a small, rocky island in the distance. The wall of jungle on their left ended abruptly, replaced by swamp and a forest of mangrove trees. Harriet stopped the cart.

She heard Mark sniff the air beside her. "Smells like rotten eggs," he said. He sniffed again. "I take that back. It smells like something died in there mixed with rotten eggs."

"There are large carnivorous plants in the swamp that entice their prey with the scent of dead meat. To some creatures it's as attractive as the finest perfume," Solly said. "Be thankful the smell doesn't reach our cottages."

The buzz of insects filled the air. A bellow sounded from deep in the swamp, making Harriet shudder. The saltwater crocs terrified her. They grew to twenty feet in length, weighed more than two thousand pounds, and were at the top of the food chain on the island. Anything–including humans–was potentially a tasty treat. They were indiscriminate hunters.

"Let's spread out and search the edges of the swamp." Harriet pulled off her sneakers. "It's too dangerous to go into the interior."

"If Okido ventured in there she's already become some-body's meal and we'll never find her." Solly jumped out of the cart. "Let's get this done."

Harriet began to wade among the mangrove roots looking for a body with blue hair. The shallow water had been warmed by the sun to nearly bath temperature. Small crabs and fish darted around her feet and tickled her toes and ankles. She glanced toward Mark to see how he was doing. Was his blade waterproof? Would the saltwater rust it? She wanted to ask but the man was so easily offended she didn't dare.

"She's not here," Mark called after twenty minutes. "Where to next?"

"We head north; search the greenhouses, laundry, garage and the areas around them," Solly answered, heading for the cart. He slid into the driver's seat ahead of

Harriet and stuck his tongue out at her when she climbed into the back.

"Brat."

"Sticks and stones," Solly replied with a grin.

They enlisted the workers at each building to help them look. The search of the greenhouses and other buildings went quickly and turned up nothing. By the time they finished Harriet's stomach was making hungry noises and she suggested they return to the cottages, eat, and contact Alex with what they had so far.

"Which is nothing," Mark pointed out.

"Not true. We've eliminated places where Okido might be, so that's something," Harriet argued. "We're narrowing the search area."

Mark pressed his lips together. "All right. I'll concede that turning up nothing could be considered progress of a sort. And I definitely could eat. Should we try the canteen? I haven't checked my chiller yet to see what's in there."

"The canteen sounds great. I need to shower and put on clean clothes." Solly parked in front of Mermaid. "Meet back at the cart in thirty? That enough time for you, Harry?"

"I'll be ready before either of you clowns." Harriet hopped out of the cart and rushed to her door. "Time starts *now!*" She disappeared inside, leaving Solly and Mark still sitting in the cart.

"No way we can let her beat us," Mark said.

"Better hurry then. Harry can shower and change faster than you'd think possible."

The two men jumped from the cart and ran to their cottages. Mark could hear water running inside Mermaid and found himself grinning again as he raced to take his own shower and change.

CHAPTER TEN

Harriet was sitting in the driver's seat with a smug smile on her face when Solly and Mark emerged from their respective cottages. Solly gave her The Look, one he'd perfected during their years of rooming together, a look he used whenever she irritated him or he wanted her to think he was irritated. She always got such pleasure out of believing she'd gotten to him that sometimes he played it up just to see her response.

"Took you two long enough." Harriet's grin widened when she saw Solly's face.

"I think you cheated. Your hair is dry." Solly climbed in the front. Harriet stuck her tongue out at him and took off as soon as Mark settled in the back.

Mark listened to the pair's banter on the way to the canteen. He had no sisters and had never had a friends-only relationship with a woman. Up until his relationship with Miriam he had assumed that women were for wining and dining with the end goal of having sex. He hadn't known that friendship was possible. Looking back, he saw that he hadn't known Miriam at all. He had been dazzled by her, but he hadn't known her.

He felt a twinge of envy over Solly's relationship with Harriet. The two were obviously close and easy with one another. Would he ever have that in his own life? He put the topic away to think about later when he was alone.

Alex and Fox tracked them down at the canteen halfway through their meal. Alex pulled an extra chair from a nearby table and set it next to Harriet. Despite the fact that the canteen was busy, the waitress came right away and both men ordered. Word had gotten out about Alicia Wynn's death. The other diners were looking at their table and whispering.

"I'm so hungry I'm hallucinating the smell of a Boston sausage and pepper sandwich from Funicelli's," Fox said, after the waitress had left to relay their order to the chef. "I must have missed lunch."

"Did Dr. Clarke and . . . Alicia get off okay?" Harriet asked. She couldn't bring herself to refer to Alicia Wynn as the body. It felt too disrespectful toward a person who had once paved the way for women to hold positions of power in the film industry.

Alex snitched a crab-stuffed mushroom from her plate. "They left for the mainland an hour ago. Eleanor said she'd do the autopsy tonight and return in the morning." He popped the mushroom into his mouth and eyed another. Harriet put up a hand to shield her plate.

"Your food is coming. Leave mine alone. We worked up an appetite looking for Okido. Speaking of, unless she's lost in the jungle or wandered into the middle of the mangrove swamp, we've eliminated the south end of the island."

"You didn't want to risk a kisser to kisser with a salt-water croc?" Fox asked. His bright green eyes sparkled with humor in his handsome, tanned face. An inveterate flirt, Fox was a favorite with the resort's female employees. He had also become a good friend to Harriet.

"The crocs scare the bejeezus out of me," she admitted.

"We spoke to Dirk Haywood. We thought it might help our search if we knew more about Okido." Solly finished the last of his shrimp scampi and pushed away his plate. "Did you know that she was a stunt double before she became his PA? Apparently he didn't hire her; Alicia did. Dirk's long time assistant left and he was too busy to conduct interviews so Alicia took care of it."

"A stunt double?" Alex looked at Fox. "Did you know that?" Fox shook his head.

"First I've heard of it."

The waitress brought two plates heaping with food and set them in front of Fox and Alex, along with a broad wink for Fox. "Chef says you both get extra because he knows you're working hard. Bon appétite."

Neither man wasted any time digging into their meals. Alex devoured half his plate before he slowed enough to speak again. "Did you learn anything else about Okido from Haywood?"

"He thought that she might prefer women to men," Mark answered. "No proof, but he never saw Okido in the company of a man–although I'm not sure if that means anything. Okido might simply have preferred to keep her private life private."

"It helps build a picture of the woman we're looking for," Alex told him. "It was smart of you to speak with Haywood."

Harriet waited for Mark to acknowledge that it had been her idea but he kept quiet. Putz.

"What's next?" Fox pushed away his empty plate and drained his beer. "If Okido was a stunt double she should know how to take care of herself. Are we looking for a woman who's been abducted, or–god forbid–killed, or are we looking for someone who is hiding?"

"Why would she be hiding?" Harriet asked. "She disappeared the day before Alicia went missing. I heard Alicia accuse Dirk of sending her away. You talked to Alicia, Alex. Did she tell you why she thought Dirk might have sent Okido away?"

"She did accuse him of sending Okido home, yes. But we checked with the shuttle crews and no one has left the island since the current group of guests arrived."

"So she's still on the island." Her appetite gone, Harriet pushed her plate away. Fox and Alex immediately grabbed the last of her stuffed mushrooms and put them on their own plates. "We searched the amusement park, the spa, and were about to search Morgan's cove when you called to say Alicia had been found. Do you want us to finish searching the pirate coves?"

"We only have another hour of daylight left," Alex said. "The pirate coves can wait until morning. It would be great if you could search them then. I honestly don't think she's there, but they need to be eliminated. We've already searched the circus and shuttle area. Fox and I will search the hotel and check the employee housing before we quit for the night. I need to search Alicia's rooms and speak with Haywood again."

"Sounds like a busy night," Mark said. "Are you sure we can't do more to help?"

"Not tonight. I appreciate you stepping up. Tomorrow morning we'll inform the guests that we're looking for Okido and ask that anyone who saw her before she disappeared file a report at the security office stating when and where she was seen. We'll build a timeline of her movements and see if any ideas pop from there."

Mark stood. "Well, it sounds as if you have things well in hand. I'm going to head for my cottage and catch up on some reports." He looked at Solly. "When do you want to head out tomorrow?"

Solly looked at Harriet. "You want to run first thing tomorrow?"

"No. I'll save my energy for the search. We'll head for the pirate coves at seven. Most of the guests should still be in then."

"Good enough. I'll meet you out front at seven." Mark wove his way through the tables and disappeared inside the canteen. Harriet watched him go. His limp was more pronounced than it had been earlier in the day. She wondered if his leg bothered him more when he got tired and felt a twinge of sympathy that she instantly suppressed. The man obviously didn't like her. She wasn't going to waste any sympathy on him.

Solly stood also. "I'm going to swing by the kitchens. I'll catch you in the morning, Harry. Later, Fox. Alex."

"Why is Solly headed to the kitchens?" Fox asked.

"He and the new pastry chef have become an item. They're keeping it on the down-low because Chef William is recently out of a bad marriage and he doesn't want word to get back to his ex that he's happy. Apparently he's afraid the ex could be vindictive."

"Afraid the ex will pitch a boogie-woogie? That's too bad. I hope things work out for him and Solly. Solly's an in-there cat."

Harriet gave Fox a puzzled look. "Solly's a what? A cat?"

Fox tossed his napkin on the table and stood. "In-there. Likable. A good person. Sincere. He's a stand-up guy in other words. I see someone I want to talk to. I'll meet you out front, Alex. Later, Harry." He planted a kiss on her cheek and headed for the table where Tamara, the attractive circus gatekeeper he'd been recently dating had just sat down.

Alex hitched his chair closer to Harriet's. "You doing okay?" he asked. He pushed her hair behind her shoulder and rubbed her neck. Harriet leaned into his warm, calloused hand.

"Other than being upset about Alicia and worried that Okido might be dead too and the fact that my employer's CFO hates me? Yeah, I'm doing all right."

"I can't do anything about Alicia and Okido, but for what it's worth I don't think Fortner hates you. How could anyone hate you?" He leaned in for a lingering kiss. "Sorry about the recent sleeping arrangements," he said when he pulled away. "Have you heard from Dr. Bainbridge?"

"No, but Payson has. The good Dr. Bainbridge has narrowed the field of mad doctors down to three suspects and is hunting for them now."

"Are you worried?"

Harriet considered for a moment, then shook her head. "I've been too busy to even think about it, to be honest. Alex, do you think Okido is dead too? And if she is, would that mean that Dirk Haywood is the killer? He claims that he and Alicia had smoothed out their differences right before she disappeared, but–"

"Did you believe him?"

Harriet thought for a moment. "Yes. Yes, I did. But then he's an award winning actor. How do I know what's real and what isn't?"

"That's the rub, isn't it?" Alex stood and pulled Harriet to her feet by her hand, placed a chaste kiss on her cheek. "I have to get back to it. Call me tomorrow after you've searched the pirate coves."

"You'll call if you find anything?"

"I promise. Take a cart home. You've been on your feet long enough."

Alex was right; her legs and feet were tired. Luckily, there was a cart conveniently parked in front of the canteen. Harriet decided to take Alex's advice; she hopped into the cart and headed to Mermaid cottage. She'd thought she was tired enough to go straight to bed, but poured herself a glass of wine and slipped out to her lanai to watch the sun set instead.

Other than a pod of dolphins arcing gracefully through the water in the last rays of the sun, the beach was quiet. Even the gulls and pipers had gone to roost wherever shorebirds spent the night. Small waves broke softly on the sand and retreated. The breeze had lessened to a gentle caress on her face. The scent of the night-blooming jasmine on Solly's lanai perfumed the air.

If she only considered the present moment, she lived in a beautiful, peaceful paradise and her life was perfect. What did anyone have but the present moment? Life couldn't be lived in the past or the future. There was only the now.

Harriet settled lower on her chaise lounge and sighed. Some of her fellow employees had nicknamed the resort "Destination Death" after the second death on the island and the news feeds had picked up the moniker. She had been furious at first, but now? Now she had to wonder what it was about the resort that made it a destination for people with evil on their mind.

Alicia Wynn. Despite her recent box office flops the woman had still been a major player in Hollywood. Because of Alicia's outspoken views and her willingness to hire women for the highest positions, the industry was no longer a bastion run by men. Her death was a big deal and would affect many. Could a jealous someone from the industry have wanted her dead? Or could Dirk Haywood have killed his wife? Everyone knew that a large percentage of murders were committed by people close to the victim.

She had never seen or heard any gossip claiming the actor to be a womanizer. From all appearances he appeared to be genuinely upset over his wife's death. Then again, as she had told Alex, the man was a skilled actor. He could project any emotion he wanted on demand.

Still, she couldn't help but think that it made no sense for him to bring his wife and personal assistant to the resort only to kill them. No, Dirk was not their killer, she felt sure of it.

Pulling her link from her pocket, she tagged Alex. "It's me," she said, when he answered. "Have you checked to see if any of the guests are linked to Hollywood or the film industry in any way? I honestly don't believe that Dirk is the killer."

Alex gave an exasperated sigh. "One step at a time. We don't know yet how Alicia Wynn died. She could have gone for a late night swim, hit her head, and drowned. And yes, I'll be checking the guest list for any connections. Let it go. Get some sleep. Good night, Harriet." He cut her off.

"What makes you believe Haywood is innocent?"

Harriet started, sloshing wine over her hand. She hadn't even looked over at Persephone's lanai, hadn't realized that Mark was out there.

"I thought you were working." How long had he been standing there? Had he been watching her the whole time? Complete darkness had descended with the sunset. It was one of the things about tropical living that she hadn't grown accustomed to. In New England there was a long stretch of twilight before sunrise and after sunset. In the tropics the sunset was like someone had suddenly switched off the light. One minute she could see, the next her eyes were adapting to the dark.

"I couldn't concentrate." He didn't wait for an invitation. He limped across the sandy strip between the two cottages and climbed the two steps onto Harriet's lanai and settled onto the lounger next to Harriet's.

"I couldn't help overhearing your call to Alex. You think Alicia might have been targeted because of her position in Hollywood?"

Harriet didn't even try to keep the bitchiness from her tone. "You shouldn't eavesdrop. It's not polite."

"It was hard to avoid," Mark said mildly. "You're only twenty feet away and it's quiet here. Besides, I learn a lot by eavesdropping. Can you say that you've never done it? Either accidentally or on purpose? What did Alex think of your idea?"

"He'd already considered it," Harriet admitted. She took a sip of her wine. She knew she should tell Mark she was going to bed and head inside, but she found that she didn't want to. She wanted the company. She felt unsettled by Alicia's death. Normally she would talk to Solly about it but he was busy. Alex was busy. Fox was with Alex and this wasn't something she wanted to bother Cassie with. There wasn't anyone else.

"No, I don't think Dirk Haywood is a killer," she finally said. It was easier to talk in the dark, knowing Mark couldn't see her face. "Nothing about the situation makes any sense to me at the moment, but I feel sure Dirk isn't responsible for Okido's disappearance or Alicia's death."

"I agree with you."

"You do? That's . . . surprising. I was under the impression you would disagree with anything I might say."

"Come on, I haven't been that bad, have I?" When

Harriet didn't answer, Mark sighed. "If I have, then I apologize."

Harriet let the apology sit between them without acknowledging it. She sipped her wine and let the peaceful evening wash over her while she waited to see what Mark would do or say next. He didn't keep her waiting long.

"Did Solly tell you how I lost my foot?"

The question was unexpected. She looked over, saw his eyes glittering in the starlight. He was looking at her. "No. Why? Did you expect him to?"

"You two are such good friends, I guess I assumed that he would share whatever I told him with you."

"Friendship doesn't mean either of us would break a confidence. Would you like to tell me about it?" She had to admit she was curious. Some of the scars on Mark's leg were still an angry red; a sure indication that whatever had happened was fairly recent.

Mark felt a flutter of panic in his chest. Did he want Harriet to know how stupid he'd been? She thought little enough of him as it was. Despite his misgivings, he decided that he *would* like to tell her. He repeated the story, answered Harriet's questions, and was surprised to realize that it was easier telling this time around. She didn't make him feel stupid for trusting Miriam; on the contrary, she railed against Miriam's deceit. He even smiled at the string of expletives she applied to his ex.

"I can't wrap my head around some of the things people will do to one another," she finished. "Mr. Wade did the right thing sending you here. The island is a good place to heal body and soul. Despite the murders."

She fell silent as she thought about how true that was. They were both quiet for a while. She was beginning to think Mark had fallen asleep when he spoke.

"I take it you and Alex are an item?"

"We're engaged to be married. Well, actually we're not engaged, not yet, but we will be, once . . . once some personal issues on my part are straightened out."

Mark waited, hoping his silence would prompt Harriet to tell him about the personal issues, but she stood and excused herself, claiming she needed to go to bed. He remained on her lanai until the lights inside the cottage went on, then made his way back to Persephone.

The more time he spent with Harriet the more attractive she became. If he was smart he would excuse himself from the search tomorrow and focus on the job he came to do. He had no business messing with Alex's woman. Alex was a decent man and Mark had never been one to poach another man's mate.

He went to bed knowing that he had every intention of meeting her and Solly at seven.

CHAPTER ELEVEN

The next morning Harriet set the security alarm for the cottage before joining Solly and Mark who were already waiting in a cart. She'd had trouble sleeping after Mark had told her about Miriam's deceit and the bomb she had placed in his office. She didn't want to like Mark–he was arrogant and rude and he didn't need or want her sympathy–but the more time she spent with him the better she understood him, and the better she understood Mark the more she liked him.

Usually that wouldn't be a problem for her–she liked people in general. Liking Mark wasn't something that should keep her awake. But the fact that she also felt a growing attraction to him was a different–and disturbing–kettle of fish. She loved Alex. She wanted to marry Alex. She shouldn't feel attracted to another man. What did that say about her character? Did feeling attracted to two men mean she was fickle? Or was she turning into a loose woman?

Worrying about the state of her morals had kept her tossing and turning through most of the night. She should have just admitted that she couldn't sleep and started the day earlier with her usual run. Instead, she'd forced herself to stay in bed and as a consequence felt tired and grumpy.

Mark gave her a curt nod from behind the wheel but said nothing. So much for their tête-à-tête the previous night. Apparently they were back to playing it cool and distant. Fine. She would play his game. She climbed into the rear seat and glared at the back of Mark's head.

Solly raised an eyebrow when he caught her expression but merely reached back with a chocolate croissant on a neatly folded cloth napkin. "Try this. William's been experimenting. He wants to know what you think."

Harriet took a bite of the flaky pastry. All grumpy thoughts fled and she groaned with pleasure. "Oh. My. God." The contrast of the bitter, dark chocolate pastry with the delicate, light, orange flavored cream filling tasted sublime.

"This is so good. The crispy crunch of the pastry with the sweet cream—tell him these need to go on the breakfast menu as soon as possible. And he should make plenty. These will be an instant winner. They could become his signature dish—they're that good. Oh! You know what? I'm going to put them in the new ad I'm working on."

Solly smiled with pleasure. "William will be thrilled."

"Enough about food." Mark started the cart and headed toward the main resort. "Where to first?"

"Back to Morgan's Cove," Solly instructed. "We never searched it yesterday. We'll work our way north and hit the four pirate coves, then check with Alex to see if he wants us to search the north end of the island."

"Morgan's it is."

No longer grumpy, Harriet enjoyed the ride to Morgan's Cove. The three jungle-covered mountains that created the island's spine cast the quiet shell road in shadow that time of morning. She imagined the insects and reptiles that inhabited the island frozen in place, waiting for the sun's rays to warm them so they could go about their daily business of hunting for food and attracting mates.

The day shift was already hard at it in the kitchens. In contrast, the offices were quiet at that time of morning. A few early risers sat on the benches in front of the hotel. A lone figure jogged down the beach at the water's edge where the sand was packed hard by the receding tide. Mark took the left-hand fork and passed the spa, then turned down the lane to Morgan's Cove.

Since all the cottages on the southernmost pirate cove were filled with families with children, they were all bustling with activity even at the early hour. Harriet wondered if the parents ever wished for a sleep-in while on vacation, or if they were happy to entertain their children as soon as they crawled out of their beds. She made a mental note to do some research–maybe the resort should offer a pajama party for kids one night a week to give the parents a break.

Soon she sat in the kitchen of a three bedroom cottage, questioning the parents while three children aged from pre-teen to toddler told Solly about their plans for the day. Mark stood just inside the door looking out of place and antsy.

The parents appeared sleepy but relaxed. It was plain to see that this was a solid, happy family.

What had her own parents been like? Were they as patient with her as this couple was with their children? Did they like to take her to see new places? She tried to recollect any memory of their life together before their untimely deaths. There was nothing but a searing pain that tore suddenly through her skull. The mother gave her a concerned look when she groaned.

"I'm okay," she whispered, closing her eyes. "Just give me a moment." Dr. Bainbridge had counseled her to think of something pleasant and current whenever her efforts to remember brought on the pain. She pictured her run on the beach the previous morning and the pain disappeared, almost like a switch had been turned off.

She opened her eyes, blinked, and took a few breaths to steady herself. Mark and Solly were both watching her.

"Sorry about that. I thought I was getting a migraine but it's gone."

"Oh, I have a friend who suffers from those," said the wife, a pretty, tanned blonde in her mid-thirties. "She used to spend an entire day in bed with the black-out shades drawn. Her doctor prescribes something to help make them less debilitating and it's helped her a lot. I can call her if you like and see what she takes."

Harriet smiled. "That's very kind of you, but I'll be okay. I'm working with a specialist who is confident he can help me. So, neither of you have seen this woman since you arrived?"

No one had seen the lady with blue hair in the cove, although several adults had seen Okido days before. Harriet made a note of the times and locations of the sightings to give Alex later. After interviewing the guests they searched the entire beach and area surrounding the cottages.

"This will take all day at this rate," Mark said. "We need a more efficient game plan."

"What do you suggest?" Harriet had discreetly watched Mark navigate the terrain around the cove in case the footing proved too difficult for his prosthetic blade. Walking on the smooth level surface of a floor was far different from walking on uneven ground. He had stumbled a time or two but quickly recovered and hadn't let it slow him down.

"I think we should split up at the next cove. You handle questioning the guests while Solly and I search along the water and behind the cottages. If we split up, by the time you speak to everyone we should be finished with the search."

"Ha." She pointed a finger at his face. "Admit it–you don't want to talk to the guests." Mark leveled a look at her over his sunglasses, a look almost identical to the one Solly used when she irritated him. Harriet suppressed a grin, but inside she gave a fist pump. She'd guessed correctly and called him on it.

"I'm merely pointing out that in the name of efficiency we need to split up: one interviews, one searches along the water, and one searches around the cottages."

She couldn't fault him for not wanting to speak to the guests. The children had openly gawked at his blade and asked questions about it. One thing she had learned from spending time with her orphans–children will notice anything that is different about a person, no matter how slight, and they had no filter on what they said.

She gave Mark credit. He had been good about their questions, telling them only that he'd had an accident and explaining how his blade worked, but she had felt his discomfort at the attention. She decided to show him some mercy.

"Fine. We'll split up. It makes more sense. *But*," she paused, "We each take a different task at the last three coves. I'll interview the guests in Black Bart's. Solly will take Blackbeard's, and you do the interviews at Kidd's. And we'll switch up the search as well."

"Agreed."

Black Bart's had the sunken pirate ship and was a favorite with the teens who came to the island and wanted to dive. Because only adults and teens occupied the cottages many were still sleeping. They weren't happy to have their rest time intruded upon, although most changed their tune when they realized a woman was missing. Harriet insisted on waking and speaking with everyone staying in the cove which ate up more time than she liked.

The sun blazed high overhead in the bright blue sky and the island life had come alive by the time they finished searching the second cove. The buzz, chirp, and whir of insects created a steady soundtrack to the day. Brilliant red, blue, and green colored lizards darted through the undergrowth and up and down the trees chasing bugs. They had to stop several times for the large green iguanas who liked to sun in the road. By the time they reached the last pirate cove it was nearing lunchtime and their energy was flagging.

"I'll take the shoreline," Solly said, and took off.

"I'll search around the cabins. If you run into problems give me a shout." Harriet didn't wait for Mark's answer. Kidd's Cove was usually reserved for the older adults so questioning them wouldn't be difficult. She started checking the undergrowth behind the nearest cabin.

Snakes were common in the jungle although no poisonous snakes had been found on the island. Poisonous or not, Harriet disliked snakes intensely. She used a stout stick to poke through the dense growth. Focused on avoiding the thorny plants and biting insects, she soon forgot about Mark. It wasn't until she heard male voices coming from around the corner that she realized she had come to the last cottage, the one belonging to Payson.

She started around the corner to greet her friend but

froze when she saw Mark in what looked to be an intense conversation with the older man.

"Have you said anything to them?" Payson asked. Mark shook his head.

"I know better, although I don't know how much longer you can keep it from them. They aren't stupid. Does Hayes know? They're bound to guess eventually, you know. It would be better if you came clean first."

Harriet frowned. The two men were speaking as if they knew each other well. But then, it made sense that they would. Payson was a close friend of Douglas Wade's and Mark worked closely with Wade. They would have met at some point, especially since Payson often did things for Wade.

"I'll tell them."

"When?"

"When I'm ready. Island life is agreeing with you; you don't look as pale and washed out as you did."

"Yeah. It's a nice place."

Harriet decided she'd better make her presence known before they noticed her. She cleared her throat and approached the men.

"Hi, Payson. I see you've met Mark." She kissed Payson's cheek. He was dressed in his favorite at-home clothing—loose, lightweight, off-white linen pants and shirt. His thick white hair hung loose and touched his shoulders, his tanned feet were bare. The man managed to convey elegance and quiet power even in casual dress.

"Harry. How are you this morning? Mark says you're having no luck finding Okido."

Solly joined them in time to hear Payson's comment. "Hey, Payson. No luck yet, I'm afraid. This was the last cove to search. It's not looking good, especially after finding Alicia Wynn dead yesterday."

"If you've been searching all morning you must be hungry and thirsty. Why don't you take seats on the lanai and I'll rustle up some food and drink." Payson didn't wait for an answer. He headed inside, leaving them no choice but to sit.

"Harry! Can you help me carry this stuff out?"

Harriet was well acquainted with Payson's cottage. While only a two bedroom, it was as large as a four bedroom, with generously proportioned rooms. The warm golden-hued wood floors were covered with antique, hand knotted rugs in blues and cream. A collection of finely carved wooden masks looked down from the living room walls. Some of the masks were thousands of years old, relics from long vanished civilizations.

Payson's collection of paper books–a rarity after the cutting of trees became strictly regulated–had grown since she was last in the cottage. She stopped by the table next to his reading chair and checked out the titles of the books piled there. They ranged in subject from the diversity of coral reefs to the making of a cult.

"If you take the pitcher of lemonade and the glasses I'll bring the food," Payson called from the kitchen. Harriet replaced the book on cults where she'd found it and hurried into the kitchen. Payson's kitchen island was the most dramatic she'd ever seen, even in decorating e-zines. The kitchen's warm cherry cabinets complimented the island's deep blue granite surface and picked up the swirls of rich russet in the granite.

Payson handed Harriet the loaded tray. She set it back on the island. "You must have met Mark through Mr. Wade," she began. She wanted to ask him about the conversation she'd overheard between the two men, but admitting that she'd eavesdropped suddenly made her uncomfortable. The overheard conversation was none of her business.

"Yes. I know Mark quite well, actually." Payson seemed unaware of Harriet's discomfort.

"Right. I'd better take these out." Harriet grabbed the tray of drinks and hurried out to the lanai. Payson followed more slowly with a large tray heaped with sliced cheeses, cured sliced meats, a variety of olives and pickled mushrooms, and a loaf of sliced olive bread.

Harriet was quiet while they ate. She couldn't stop thinking about the conversation she'd overheard. What did Mark mean when he asked if Alex knew? Did Alex know what? And who were the "they" that Mark was referring to when he said they were bound to guess eventually? What did Payson have to come clean about?

She caught Payson studying her and forced a smile. Payson was shrewd, intelligent, and read her easily. He knew she had something on her mind–she could see it in his eyes. She pulled her link from her pocket before he could ask her about it and hit speed-dial.

"I'm going to call Alex and see if he wants us to continue searching," she said. "Alex. Solly, Mark, and I are with Payson. We searched all four pirate coves. No one has seen Okido in the last two days. I'm going to put you on speaker." She set the link so everyone could hear and placed it in the center of the table.

"We took notes on when and where anyone saw Okido in case you wanted to track her activity the day she disappeared," Solly said. "Any joy at your end?"

"Dr. Clarke sent the autopsy report. There was no water in Alicia's lungs so she was dead before she went into the water. We can rule out accidental death."

"Do we know when she died?" Solly asked.

"Between ten and two the previous night, best guess.

Eleanor couldn't be more precise because crabs had eaten Alicia's eyes."

Harriet pushed her plate away. "Too much information."

"Ah jeez. Sorry, Harriet. I wasn't thinking."

Solly shot Harriet a sympathetic look. "Do you want us to search the north end of the island? We've checked the road edges and along the shore of each cove, but the jungle is too thick to do a proper search. We might need to bring in dogs if you want to search the island's interior."

"No, come back. I'll run up there on my bike even though my gut tells me it's a waste of time."

"What are you thinking, Alex?" Payson asked. "Are we looking for another body?"

"I certainly hope not, but we're into the third day since Okido went missing and it doesn't look good." Harriet heard Fox's voice rumble in the background. "I have to go. Haywood is here insisting that we take him to see his wife. Go back to the office. I'll let you know if I need your help again." He cut the connection and Harriet slipped the link back into her pocket.

"I guess we head back to the office." Alicia's eyes were gone. What else had the crabs eaten? No wonder Leonard had looked ill after he'd seen her body. Harriet firmly pushed the mental image away and stood. "I'll help you clean up, Payson."

Payson waved off her offer. "I have it." Harriet hesitated. It wasn't right to leave Payson with the mess after he'd fed them.

"Go. I mean it." Solly and Mark thanked Payson for the meal and headed for the cart at the other end of the cove.

Now was not the time to ask Payson about the conversation she'd overheard. It was none of her business.

"Thanks for lunch." She kissed him on the cheek. "I'll see you next Thursday if not before." She stepped off the lanai.

"Harriet."

"Yes?" Payson never called her Harriet, not since she'd given him permission to call her Harry.

Payson shook his head. "Never mind. It's not the right time." He gathered up the dirty dishes and disappeared inside the cottage. Harriet waited for a few moments, then turned away and headed for the cart.

Not the right time for what?

CHAPTER TWELVE

"Dr. Edgar Bainbridge to see Dr. Cliff Miles, please."

The receptionist directed Edgar through a door where he found an opulent waiting room that smelled of sandalwood and rich coffee. Passing the deep maroon leather club chairs set on a gold and white patterned oriental, he crossed to the large windows that looked out over the Thames and clasped his hands behind his back. He had no doubts that Miles would see him–out of curiosity if nothing else.

He was really hoping that Miles would turn out to be the person he was looking for. If not–he suppressed a shudder. If not, he would have to deal with someone he'd hoped never to have to see again.

Below him on the walking path a man dressed in athletic shorts and a sweatshirt with the arms cut off stopped to tie his shoe. One half of his body was covered with elaborate tats, the other half was naked. A young couple jogged by, the man pushing a three-wheeled stroller. A dog walker struggled to untangle the four leashes she held. Edgar wondered if they were her dogs or if she was a professional walker. A bright yellow rowing scull flew over the water close to shore, its two man crew in perfect sync.

"Ed. What brings you to London?"

Edgar turned from the window and blinked with surprise. Miles had always been attractive; now he looked almost film-idol handsome. He examined the changes: brown eyes now a deep violet courtesy of colored lenses, a stronger chin with a shallow cleft dividing it, sharper cheekbones. He had traded his Roman nose for a narrower, straighter version. His bleached hair, artfully arranged in tufts as if he had just run his hands through it, set off tanned skin.

It was dispiriting to realize that Miles looked twenty years younger than he did even though they were the same age.

"You've had work done," he blurted out, then flushed with embarrassment. He had always felt a sort of unspoken rivalry with Miles, but Miles merely smiled. His violet eyes sparkled with suppressed humor.

"Yes, well. It seemed the prudent thing to do at the time." He casually waved a hand, encompassing the waiting room and the view out the windows. "As you can see, I've quite recovered from that little incident with the Russian diplomat. What can I do for you? Since I haven't seen or spoken with you since graduation day I assume you looked me up for a specific reason."

"I did. Could we speak somewhere private?"

Miles looked pointedly around the empty waiting room. "Sure. My office." He led the way through a heavy wooden door carved with alchemical signs and down a short hall. Original artwork decorated the hall's dark maroon walls. Thick, deep gold carpet deadened any sound their shoes might have made as they walked in silence.

"Through here."

The office was twice the size of the large waiting room, done in the now familiar maroon and gold color scheme. One entire wall was filled with windows looking out over the river. Pleasure boats wove their way around three tugs pushing barges up the middle of the channel, sending up rooster tails of spray; some close enough for Edgar to clearly make out the people onboard. To the north, Renzo Piano's Shard glowed with the sun's reflection.

Miles took the large leather chair behind a massive cherrywood desk. He didn't offer Edgar a seat. Steepling his long, slender fingers, he pursed his lips.

"What is this concerning, Ed? I have a client due in twenty minutes and I need time to prep."

So, this wasn't going to be as cordial as Edgar had hoped. Fine. Despite the fact that Miles had made a point of not inviting him to sit, Edgar settled in the client chair in front of the desk and crossed his legs.

"Twenty years ago a woman by the name of Wendolyn Wainwright took her eight year old niece to see a head doctor in order to have the niece's memories wiped. The niece is now in her late twenties and would like her memories returned."

Miles's eyes lit with interest. He leaned forward in his chair. "Do tell."

"I wondered if Ms. Wainwright might have been your client, and if so, can you tell me if the process can be reversed."

"What an interesting problem. Wiping the memories of a child." Miles shook his head. "The memories must have been quite traumatic for the aunt to take such a drastic measure. An interesting problem indeed. And quite unethical I believe. Does one person, even an adult, have the right to take the memories from another? Do you know why the child's memories were wiped?"

"No. Nor would I tell you if I did. Is this something you might have done?" Miles's grin reminded Edgar of the wolf in Red Riding Hood.

"Oh, it's definitely something I might have done if I'd had the opportunity. In this case I'm afraid it's not something that I did do, however." He sat back in his chair. "I'm rather envious of the person who did. Who else have you asked?"

"Audra Stinson. Like you she had some, uh, difficulties in her career, and has changed her name."

"Audra Stinson." Miles snapped his fingers. "Her specialty was essentially brain surgery using an electron-wide laser beam. She showed up for surgery hungover and slipped. Am I remembering right?"

"Yeah." Edgar pushed himself out of the chair. "I'd best be going."

Miles walked him to the office door. He stood with his hand on the knob, his brow furrowed. Standing that close in a beam of sunlight, Edgar could see the tiny scars from the face work. A top professional would have left no scar tissue. He smiled inwardly. The scars meant that Miles had been forced to seek out a lesser surgeon for the reconstruction work, presumably as part of turning himself into Cliff Miles.

How he must have hated that. Miles had always insisted on the best of everything when they'd been at school. The thought buoyed Ed's mood.

Thanks for your time, Miles."

"It's Cliff now. Much as I'd like to believe that my methods can do everything, aversion therapy alone couldn't wipe memories. It would be useful to prevent those memories from coming back, but it wouldn't delete them in the first place. Do you have someone else in mind? There aren't many head doctors at our level of expertise practicing."

Edgar appreciated being counted among the top practitioners. "There are only four of us still alive who were practicing twenty years ago," he said. "I have to go. I have a shuttle to catch."

He was halfway back to the waiting room when he heard Miles's hoot of laughter.

"It's bloody McDougall!" Miles called after him.

Edgar raised his hand in acknowledgement but didn't bother to turn around. Miles's laughter seemed to follow him until he exited the building.

Bloody McDougall, indeed.

CHAPTER THIRTEEN

The long sleepless night and morning's search had taken its toll on Harriet. She gave up on work after she caught herself nodding off at her desk for the third time, told Jeeves she'd be at Mermaid Cottage if anyone needed her, and set off on foot thinking the fresh air would wake her up.

Palm fronds rattled loudly over her head in the strong onshore breeze that had kicked up since she'd entered her office, spitting out the large palmetto bugs that lived in their lofty heights. The steady wind drowned out the usual peaceful sounds–sounds that were the soundtrack to her new life–the constant reminders that she now lived on a tropical island.

A coconut dropped onto the road nearly at her feet and she decided it would be safer to leave the road. Falling coconuts could knock a person unconscious, and in some cases had been known to even kill. She crossed to walk the edge of the beach but the wind picked up the fine sand and flung it at her hard enough to abrade her skin, so she dropped down to the water's edge where the sand was wet and lay where it belonged.

The seals and dolphins who habitually hunted just offshore had headed for deeper water. The outgoing tide battled the strong onshore breeze, churning the usual long swells into froth-tipped chaos. A few hardy seagulls bobbed up and down on the disordered crests. What food they hoped to find, Harriet couldn't begin to guess. Maybe they simply enjoyed the wild ride.

She stood at the water's edge in front of her cottage and embraced the stiff breeze, reveling in the way it pressed her shirt and shorts to her body and inflated her lungs. This was the first time since coming to the island that the weather had kicked up any kind of fuss. Compared to the storms, blizzards, and hurricanes she'd experienced on the Maine coast, the wind was barely worth noting, but at least it was a change from the string of perfect days she'd experienced since her arrival.

She hadn't realized how much she missed weather's variety. For the first time, she wondered if it was entirely possible to have too much of a good thing.

The beach was deserted except for a lone figure headed toward her from the southern tip of the island. Harriet watched the figure break into a jog, noted the uneven stride, and realized that she was watching Mark out for a run. He hadn't noticed her yet and she used the opportunity to study him.

The uneven gait was the result of the blade. It had flex and spring and launched Mark's body further than his natural foot did. She saw him adjust the power he gave to the left leg and the gait smoothed out. She smiled, knowing instinctively that this was the first time he had pushed himself to run since the bombing.

Afraid of his reaction if he saw her watching him, she

headed toward her cottage. She had intended to get inside before Mark caught up with her, but her movement caught his attention.

"Harriet!"

Harriet pretended she hadn't heard him, but he shouted her name again. To ignore him felt beyond rude. She stopped and waited for him to catch up with her.

"I couldn't concentrate on numbers," Mark said, stopping beside her. A light sheen of sweat and sand mixed with the mat of dark brown hair on his bare chest. Harriet averted her eyes, but not before she'd noticed that Mark looked strong and fit, even after what must have been a hellacious year focused on recovery. "I keep thinking about Okido and wonder where she could be, you know?"

"I kept nodding off at my desk," Harriet admitted. "I was going home to take a nap but the wind revived me."

Mark fell into step beside her. "Give me fifteen minutes to shower and then come to my place. I had some food delivered today. I'll rustle us up a meal and we can brainstorm about Okido."

Harriet hesitated. It really wasn't a good idea for her to spend time alone with Mark. What would Alex think? She looked up and saw that he was watching her. Here in the bright light she could see that his eyes weren't black like she'd originally thought; they were a warm, deep brown with a black rim.

"I'd like that. I'll bring wine and dessert." She suppressed a groan. What was wrong with her? She opened her mouth to give an excuse, any excuse, but Mark grinned.

"Great. See you in a bit." He hosed the sand from his body and disappeared inside Persephone.

"Harriet, you idiot. How hard would it have been to say,

'Not today, Mark, but thanks. How about a raincheck on that?'"

Harriet passed through her bedroom into the generous bath. The tongue and groove mahogany paneling used throughout the rest of the cottage had been carried into the bath as an accent to the pale ivory marble floors and walls. A mosaic of one-inch tiles covered the curved ceiling–a finely wrought portrait of a mermaid with long, flowing blonde hair sat on a rock surrounded by the sea. The small, carved plaque over her front door showed a smaller version of the same scene: Mermaid Cottage's mermaid.

Without giving it too much thought, Harriet stripped out of her clothes, put up her hair so it wouldn't get wet, and took a quick shower. She pulled on a pale rose, silk tee and faded jeans and decided to forego shoes. Five minutes later she knocked on Persephone's door.

Mark answered the door clad only in snug, worn jeans. A towel hung from his neck. Water droplets glistened on his broad, muscled chest and shoulders. Harriet swallowed and felt the heat rise in her face. She really shouldn't have come. It wasn't too late. She could still make an excuse.

"Come on in. I got hung up checking on my supply of vittles and need another minute or two." He wiped at his dripping hair with the towel and headed toward his bedroom. "I assume you know where the kitchen is," he called over his shoulder. "Go ahead and put your things in the chiller. I'll be right back."

"I really am an idiot." Harriet carried the bottle of wine and dessert into the kitchen and placed them in the chiller, then reconsidered and set the wine on the counter instead. Other than the black, white, and gray granite island, Mark's kitchen was identical to her own and Solly's. She pulled two wine glasses from a cupboard, poured the wine, and took a large gulp from her glass to fortify herself.

"I thought shrimp and pasta, if that's good with you." Mark spoke as he entered the kitchen. "Cheers." He took a sip of the wine and set the glass down. "Have a seat at the island while I wow you with my culinary expertise."

He seemed at ease in the kitchen, Harriet noted. He had pulled on a faded blue and black rugby shirt and pushed the sleeves up, revealing strong forearms. The man was obviously an athlete.

"Do you play sports?" As soon as the question popped out she wished she could take it back, but Mark didn't seem bothered.

"Rugby and squash. Just the local leagues—and I couldn't make every game, but if I was home I never missed. Mixing it up with a bunch of aggressive, macho males on the rugby field or slamming a ball in a squash court is a surprisingly effective way to burn off stress after being cooped up in an office all day looking at numbers. Here." He set salad makings and a bowl on the counter. "You can do the salad."

Harriet hunted up a cutting board and knife and went to work while Mark peeled shrimp, crushed garlic, and set a pot of water to boil. Gradually she began to relax. If she set aside her inappropriate attraction to him, cooking with Mark was a lot like cooking with Solly. They drank wine and talked about inconsequential things as the kitchen filled with the floral scent of good virgin olive oil and frying garlic.

Mark forked up a succulent shrimp and offered it to her. She popped it into her mouth. Heat from chili and the bright note of lemon blended with the sweet shrimp and garlic. "Oh yum. This is great."

"Thanks. My mother insisted I learn to cook. She

believed that no one should depend on other people to feed them and that it's lazy to live on takeout." He shrugged. "Turns out I like cooking. I find it relaxing and it serves as my one creative outlet."

"Solly says the same thing. Do you have siblings?"

"Nope. You?"

"No. Only Solly." She didn't want to talk about herself. At the same time, she didn't want to ruin what was turning into a nice evening. Time to change the subject. "So, Okido. Do you have any thoughts on where she might be?"

"Eat first. Then we'll talk."

After the dishes had been dealt with Mark topped off their glasses and picked them both up. "Let's move to the living room. It's too windy to sit on the lanai."

Harriet followed him from the kitchen. Like her own cottage, Persephone was paneled in mahogany, but any similarity ended there. Unlike the soft colors and light bamboo furniture in Mermaid, Mark's furniture was definitely masculine–large and blocky wood in the old Craftsman style, the cushions covered in greens and browns with soft red accents.

Harriet chose an armchair, afraid that if she sat on the couch Mark would sit with her. She folded her legs, tucking her bare feet beneath her.

Mark hesitated, then took the seat opposite Harriet so he could easily look at her. He hadn't expected her to accept his dinner invitation. You didn't need to be around Harriet long to know she was a person who always tried to do the right thing. He had asked, and she'd confirmed, that she and Alex Hayes were a couple and she was expecting to marry him when her brain was sorted.

He didn't know what sorting Harriet's brain entailed, but the fact that she and Alex were not engaged at the moment made him happy. The more time he spent with

Harriet, the more she fascinated him. He hadn't missed the fact that she didn't want to talk about herself. That alone intrigued him; in his experience beautiful women loved the opportunity to talk about themselves.

He wouldn't press her. He couldn't remember the last time he'd enjoyed himself with a woman as much as he enjoyed being with Harriet and he didn't want to risk scaring her off. Two spots of color appeared on Harriet's cheeks and Mark realized he was staring. He cleared his throat and took a sip of wine.

"So, here's what bothers me about Okido," he said. "The woman is memorable because of her blue hair. It's the first thing anyone mentions when I show them her picture. They either remember seeing a woman with blue hair–and they remember where and when because the hair is so memorable–or they say, 'I haven't seen a woman with blue hair.'"

"They aren't looking at Okido's face, they're looking at her hair," Harriet said thoughtfully. "That's a good point. If she was wearing a hat people might not have noticed her."

Mark drummed his fingers on the flat, wooden arm of his chair. "I keep coming back to the hair. It bugs me."

"What makes no sense to me is why Dirk Haywood would have any reason to kill his wife and personal assistant. Even if they'd both discovered some awful thing about Dirk, why would he choose to get rid of them in such a public and high profile place?"

Mark frowned. "You think he's being set up."

"I-I don't know what to think, to be honest. Alex was called out on two domestic disturbances at the hotel because Alicia and Dirk were fighting loudly enough to bother the other guests."

"So there's trouble in the marriage?"

Harriet grimaced. "On Alicia's side, it definitely looks

that way. On Dirk's side, I'm not so sure. I overheard them having a heated discussion a couple days ago while I was having lunch in the canteen. They were on the other side of the hedge so I couldn't see their faces, but I had the feeling that Dirk was puzzled by the conversation more than anything else."

"Puzzled? In what way?"

"I don't know if I can explain it. It was almost like . . . it felt as if Dirk had been given the wrong script and was trying to find his place, if that makes any sense."

Harriet sipped her wine. Between her full belly, the wine, and the comfortable chair, she had to guard against relaxing too far. She found herself looking at Mark's mouth and wondered if he was a good kisser. Horrified by the direction of her thoughts, she tore her gaze away and set her wine down. She'd definitely had enough to drink.

"Okido went missing first." Harriet stared at a painting of a flower-covered, stone villa so she wouldn't have to look at Mark. "Alex checked, and she hasn't left the island, so she must be here somewhere."

"Unless she's floating in the ocean and hasn't washed ashore yet."

Harriet's gaze darted back to Mark's face. "What an awful thought."

"People do awful things to one another."

Harriet thought of the woman Mark had planned to marry trying to blow him up. "I guess they do," she said quietly.

"I think we need to know more about Okido. Wait here." He left the room and returned a few minutes later with a hard-sided brief case. Setting it on the coffee table, he popped the top to reveal a computer that looked very similar to the one Harriet had seen in Alex's office. Access to people's personal information was strictly controlled by

Web Enforcer, a multi-national company created after identity theft became so rampant that bankruptcy threatened the very underpinnings of daily commerce.

There were, however, ways to get around WE. Law enforcement had access to personal information. Banks making loans. Credit bureaus. And apparently Mark Fortner had access. Considering he worked for the richest man in the world, it made sense.

"Does Okido have another name?" Mark asked as he logged in. "Do we even know?"

"I have no idea. I don't think so."

"Here she is." He scanned the screen. "Grew up around the movie industry. Single mother who worked as a make-up artist for two different studios. Okido took gymnastic classes as a kid, started in set design, did a short stint in make-up, then tried out to be Celia Haver's stunt double for her role in *Rise of the Magis* and got the job. Worked until she quit after one of the stunt men she worked with hit a wall and was paralyzed from the waist down. Worked for Dirk as his personal assistant the last three years."

He flipped the lid shut and sat back in his chair. "Does that help us any?"

"I don't know. No. Maybe."

"All right. Let's try this: is there anyplace on the island that hasn't been searched?"

Harriet thought for a bit. "Alex and Tarbell searched the parts of the resort that we didn't get to. But . . . wait a minute." She pulled her link from her pocket and tried calling Alex but the call went to voicemail. She placed a second call.

"Tarbell, it's Harry. Mark and I were sitting here trying to decide where to search next for Okido and I wondered if you and Alex had searched the cottages on the island's east side." She listened for a minute, then said goodbye and shoved her link back in her pocket.

"Well?"

"Alex had planned to search the east side of the island this afternoon but he had to go to the mainland and he's stuck there until the wind abates. Tarbell can't leave the main resort while Alex is on the mainland in case something happens. He says if we want to search the east side he'll give us the master for the cottages. Only one is occupied so they won't take long to search. We'll have to take one of the Hogs and the interior road. Guests usually use a boat to get there but the sea's too rough at the moment and expected to get rougher."

"Do we have enough daylight left to search today?"

"We'll take flashlights just in case. Or we can put it off until morning." She knew it would be wiser to wait until morning but a sense of urgency had filled her. What if Okido was hurt and hanging on in the hope that help would eventually come? If she was hurt and lying somewhere outside, another night spent waiting for help might be too late for her.

Mark locked the computer case and stood. "I vote we go. Grab sturdy boots and something warm to put on in case we get caught out after sunset. I'll meet you out front."

Harriet grabbed the wine glasses and headed for the kitchen with them. "Don't forget to bring a flashlight!" she hollered. She let herself out and ran across the strip of sand to Mermaid.

The sun hung low and red in the sky, much lower than she had realized. Without the rays of the sun to warm it, the sand already felt cool on her bare feet. They had less than two hours to search the cottages on the east side of the island before night fell. She'd never been there, nor on the road that cut across the island, although she knew where to pick it up.

She threw a long sleeved tee over her silk tee, put on thick socks and her boots, grabbed a sweater and a jacket. She was partway out the door before she remembered the flashlight. She ran through her cottage again, stuffing snacks and drinks into the worn canvas pack she used as a pocketbook.

Mark was waiting outside in a cart when she exited the cottage. She saw that he had tossed a small pack and a flashlight in the back seat. Harriet tossed her pack in the back with his and climbed in. The wind whipped tendrils of her hair loose from her hasty braid. She did her best to corral it and keep it out of her eyes but gave up. Thinking to run back inside for a scarf or a cap, she lifted a foot out of the cart at the same moment Mark put it into gear.

"Let's go. We're burning daylight."

CHAPTER FOURTEEN

The wind continued to intensify, turning palm trees into inside-out umbrellas and sending small creatures and the resort guests scurrying for cover. Harriet and Mark watched a cook carrying a large stock pot from the kitchens to the canteen lose his toque to the greedy wind. The toque tumbled away as if the hounds of hell were after it and disappeared from sight.

Tarbell was waiting for them outside the security office when they drove up. "I don't think this is a good idea," he said, frowning at Harriet. "I tried to reach Alex but he's incommunicado. There's not many chimes until sunset and you don't want to be caught on the interior road after dark, especially in a storm. I can't cover all spots–if something goes wrong you'll be on your own."

"Have faith, Fox." Mark climbed from the cart and grabbed his pack and flashlight from the rear. "Harriet and I can take care of ourselves. Someone has to search the east side cottages. What if Okido is there and hurt? She's been missing going on three days. Another day could mean the difference between finding her alive–or not." Mark held his hand out for the keys dangling from Tarbell's fingers.

Ignoring Mark's outstretched hand, Tarbell glared at Harriet. "If anything happens to you, Alex will bust my duster. He'll have my ass in a sling, Harry. Not to mention how upset I'll be."

Touched by her friend's concern Harriet gave the Irishman a quick kiss on the cheek. "Nothing will happen, Tarbell. Mark's right. You know that someone has to search the east cottages. We're the only ones available so you might as well let us help. Give us the keys." She wiggled her fingers.

But Tarbell wasn't giving up so easily. "Where's Solly? At least take him with you. I'll feel better if there are three of you."

"Solly's tied up and can't leave. We're it. There's no one else available."

"Dammit." Tarbell handed the keys to Mark with a scowl. He pointed out the master key for the cottages. "There are supplies in all the cottages. Don't try to drive the interior road after dark. Call me if you run into any trouble."

"We'll deal with it if we do," Mark said, taking the keys. "Calling you won't do anything but make you worry. We'll be fine, Fox. I promise I'll watch out for Harriet."

Harriet resented being talked about as if she were some delicate flower that needed to be coddled. At the same time, she was beginning to have reservations about the wisdom of setting off over the interior road this late in the day. Unfortunately, she knew she wouldn't sleep worrying about Okido lying hurt somewhere and waiting for help. They had to go.

Tarbell waved them off with a troubled look on his

face. Ten minutes later they turned off the resort road onto the interior road.

"I can see why no sane person would drive this after dark." Mark downshifted and guided the Hog into a steep dip and up the other side. "This is not a road for the faint of heart."

"Alex told me that it was built for the researchers who come to study the jungle and catalogue the flora and fauna. They need access to the island's interior for that, but Mr. Wade didn't want them hacking and slashing wherever they felt like it. The road helps minimize any damage to the jungle."

They had been driving close to twenty minutes. The farther they drove from the resort, the more the road seemed to deteriorate. The jungle had closed in on them as soon as they left the main road, blocking out most of what daylight was left. Branches, vines, and large leaves slapped at the sides of the Hog as if trying to beat them back, constant reminders that they were intruders on the island.

"Call me naive, but despite Tarbell's warning, I expected the road to be a rough version of the shell road on the west side of the island." Harriet had a death grip on the suicide handle above the passenger door. Tarbell had cautioned Mark not to drive too fast. He could have saved his breath–it was impossible to go faster than a crawl over the rough interior road. "No wonder most of the guests boat to the east side."

"I take it this is your first visit to the east cottages?"

"Yes." Before she could say more, the Hog's rear end slid sideways. Harriet gasped and closed her eyes. "This may be my one and only visit," she said between gritted teeth.

"Think of it as an adventure." Mark corrected the skid, grinned, and powered through a large puddle, sending muddy water cascading off the sides of the Hog.

"You're enjoying this!"

Mark's grin widened. "I do like a challenge. Have you noticed that we seem to be climbing in altitude?" He checked the Hog's dashboard and pointed to a dial. "There. An altimeter. We started at a few feet above sea level; now we're a thousand feet up. We must be climbing the center mountain. I wonder if the road goes to the top."

"I have no idea. Watch out!" A tree, nearly a foot in diameter, lay across the road. "What now? We can't go around it and there's no room to turn around."

"There's a chainsaw in the back along with some other tools should we need them, but this beast has power and good clearance. We'll go over it."

"Ohhh, I don't think that's a good idea."

Too late. The Hog's front tires were already climbing the tree. They dropped on the other side with a bone-jarring thud. Mark slowly pushed the Hog forward until the back tires climbed and cleared the tree.

"I knew we had the clearance." Another grin flashed white in the Hog's gloomy interior.

"Luckily for you," Harriet grumped. "There are hungry leopards in this jungle you know. And snakes and spiders. I do *not* want to have to walk out of here because you got all macho and tried something foolish."

Mark reached over and squeezed her knee. "I won't let anything happen to you," he said softly. "I promise. Trust me, okay?" He chuckled at Harriet's scowl. "Honestly? I haven't had this much fun since . . ."

The laughter went out of his voice. "Well, not since before Miriam tried to kill me." He took his hand from Harriet's knee and returned it to the steering wheel.

Harriet inspected Mark's profile. His nose had a sharp hook that reminded her of an old sepia photograph she'd once seen in the Portland Museum of Art, a photo of a proud and powerful Native American warrior. What had struck her most about the photo at the time was the self-awareness in the man's expression. She imagined that he had not only known who he was, but he had also known and honored his place among his people and the land they lived on.

How would it feel to learn that the person who loved you, the most important person in your life, was only pretending? Even worse, that they had intended to kill you all along? If it happened to her she would feel devastated. Heartbroken.

"You might as well call me Harry, all my friends do."

"Harry." Mark tried it out and shook his head. "I don't think so. It doesn't feel right. I'm not a big fan of the name Harriet either, to be honest. It doesn't suit you. When I picture a woman named Harriet I see a skinny, tightly wound, prim and proper old maid. Not a beautiful, sensuous, intelligent, warm and loving woman."

Harriet could only stare at him and blink. Where had that come from? The man was a study in contradictions. She never knew if he was going to ignore her, berate her, or be rude to her. Apparently he could also be complimentary. What game was he playing with her? She narrowed her eyes at him.

"I think I like it better when you're rude to me or ignore me. At least then I know exactly where I stand." She watched the muscle in Mark's jaw tighten.

"I need to apologize for that." He hesitated, then glanced at her.

Harriet grabbed the dash with her free hand as they hit a hole. "Keep your eyes on the road."

"You took me by surprise."

"*I* took you by surprise? What do you mean?"

Mark was quiet for so long Harriet didn't think he was going to answer.

"The first day we met." His voice was low and she had to strain to hear. "I was expecting an older, buttoned up, corporate-type businesswoman in a suit–a Harriet, in other words. I was not expecting a long-legged, barefoot goddess in a beautiful dress. You threw me off my stride and I was rude to you to cover it up."

He glanced at her, then focused again on the road. "I apologize. I behaved badly that day. I was curt and rude and I'm sorry."

They made the remainder of the trip in silence. Harriet didn't know what to say or how to act after the goddess remark and apology.

Barefoot goddess. He had likened her to a barefoot goddess.

She looked out the passenger window and frowned. Mark confused her. It had been so much easier when he was rude and arrogant. This new Mark–the Mark who paid her lovely compliments and was warm and human and acted as if he liked her–this Mark made her feel a little breathless and dizzy.

She was beginning to wish she hadn't suggested they look for Okido. She wished she had asked Solly to come with them, only he had been spending the evening with William and she hadn't wanted to ask. Solly and William were a fresh, new thing that looked to be serious and had her full support. As far as Harriet was concerned, her closest friend deserved the chance to be loved. She had never seen Solly as happy as he was with William and she felt happy for him.

Still, she wished she had called him. If she had she wouldn't be feeling awkward and tongue-tied, wondering how to respond to Mark.

The road only climbed halfway to the mountaintop, an obstacle course that barely let up. Every time they overcame one obstacle a new challenge cropped up. Twice they were forced to stop and hack thick vines out of the way before the Hog could pass. Once Harriet was certain she'd spotted a jaguar watching them from the undergrowth, but when Mark stopped for a closer look it disappeared.

Increasingly aware of the lowering sun, she felt a huge sense of relief when the road began its descent to the east coast of the island. The jungle ended abruptly a hundred yards from the water, as if a giant dozer had scraped it away from the shore, leaving only bare, solid rock behind.

"Which end do you want to start with?" Mark rested his wrists over the top of the steering wheel and peered at the dark cottages spread north and south from where they sat, jutting up from the shoreline like push pins marking the long, shallow cove on a map.

"Let's start at the north end."

"Roger that." Mark put the Hog in gear and turned left. The road disappeared almost immediately. Unlike the west side cottages, there were no pretty pink and white shell parking pads set next to each building, only large slabs of gray rock. "I think this is the end of the road. We'd better leave the Hog here and hoof it."

There were no lights burning in any of the cottages. Harriet wondered if the lone guest had headed for the main resort when the wind began to kick up. She wished she was back there herself. The water was a churning, stormy gray tipped with yellow foam. The wind whipped off pieces of the foam and flung them at the shore where they collected in the crevices and low areas.

It reminded her of the time she and Solly had hitchhiked out to Two Lights State park to watch the aftermath of Hurricane Cybil. The waves had crashed and pounded the park's rocks, sending up towering sprays of water and foam that made them laugh when it caught them. They'd been young and too dumb to realize the danger. They could have been swept off the slippery rocks at any time by a large wave.

"What?" Mark asked.

"What?"

"You were shaking your head. I can search the cottages if you'd rather stay in the Hog."

"I was just thinking about my guardian angel." Harriet reached into the back and pulled her jacket from her pack. "This should be fun. That wind must be closing in on Category One hurricane force."

Mark gave her a questioning look but didn't ask about her guardian angel. "Nah. The resort would have received a warning. This is just a big wind storm."

Harriet had to throw her body against the Hog's door to get it to open. Once outside the shelter of the vehicle, the wind pushed her back against the side of the Hog and covered her with salty spray. "You sure this isn't a hurricane?" she shouted.

Mark grinned at her over the hood of the vehicle. "We're having an adventure, remember? A story to tell your kids one day."

A story to tell her kids. There would be no children if she couldn't get her brain fixed. She pushed the thought away. There was no point in worrying about the future. She had enough to deal with in the present.

Turning her back to the wind, Harriet zipped up her jacket and pulled up and secured the hood. The wind didn't feel quite so threatening bundled inside her jacket. She pulled on her canvas pack, saw that Mark had also secured his jacket and hood, and tucked her flashlight in her pocket. They headed over the rocks toward the north-ernmost cottage.

The rocks were slippery with salt spray and the wind kept knocking them off balance. Mark grabbed Harriet's hand and guided her down off the upper rocks and closer to the cottages. "They'll block some of the wind," he explained.

Harriet was surprised to see that the east cottages could only be described as rustic. Two bedrooms each held two twin-sized beds with a single four drawer dresser set between them. There was one bathroom with a simple stall shower, no tub. The living area held four basic but comfortable chairs, no couch, and the kitchen had a two-burner gas stove, chiller and coffee maker, but no stocked Redi-Meal.

"Definitely no-frills," Mark said, poking through the kitchen cabinets. "Makes sense since these cabins were built for the researchers' use and they're required to bring their own supplies."

Harriet turned to him in surprise. "I thought these were for guests who wanted a wilder experience–away from the main resort."

Mark shook his head. "These cottages weren't in the orig-inal resort plan. Douglas couldn't keep the researchers off the island–not that he wanted to. Access is one of the stipulations of the World Wildlife Sanctuary designation. At the same time he didn't want them taking up space earmarked for the resort guests or dragging mud and who knows what through the hotel lobby and making more work for the cleaning crew.

"When they aren't in use by the researchers they're available for paying guests. As you said, those who want a wilder, less pampered experience."

"These cottages don't get cleaned?" Harriet looked

around. The place was spotless. Maybe the researchers cleaned up after themselves.

"Oh, they get cleaned. I have a special line item on the cleaning budget. The cleaners who do these cottages get double pay and a bonus because they're usually an unholy mess from what I've heard. The staff who are interested are on a rotation schedule so they all get a crack at the extra money."

"Obviously no one's been in here since the cleaners were last here. Should we move on?"

The next two cottages were also spotless with no sign that anyone had been inside after the cleaners had gone through. The sun had set by the time they headed for the fourth cottage. Clouds obscured the moon and stars. The world had narrowed down to the sound of the wind and crashing waves and the smell of salt and briny, drying seaweed.

Harriet knew the next cottage was there, but without any source of light the darkness was absolute. It felt like a living entity, surrounding her and pressing against her as tangibly as the wind. She couldn't even see Mark, although she sensed his body next to her.

"This is what it must feel like to be blind," she said. "No matter how I strain I can't see a thing." She snapped on the flashlight. Her beam caught the edge of something moving, but when she swung the beam to see what it was there was nothing there.

They entered the fourth cottage and snapped on the lights. By now they had an efficient routine worked out. Harriet checked the bathroom and kitchen while Mark scanned the bedrooms and living area. She checked the trash, felt the towels to see if they were damp from use, and looked to see if any food was missing. The cottages were stocked with coffee, tea, dry and canned goods, and a few frozen items like bread and fish.

"No sign that anyone's been here." Mark joined Harriet at the back door. "On to number five?" They locked the cottage behind them and walked toward the next.

"Did you hear that?" Harriet asked. "I thought I heard a door slam." They stood and listened for several minutes but didn't hear anything other than the wind.

"Maybe something loose got caught in the wind," Mark suggested. "If it was a door we should run into the guest who slammed it."

"Wait." Harriet grabbed Mark's arm. "Look." She played the flashlight beam over the rocks behind the cottages.

"What? I don't see anything."

"Neither do I. So where's the Hog? We left it right there, behind these two cottages."

"Shit. I left the keys in it. I'm sorry. It never occurred to me that anyone would steal it."

CHAPTER FIFTEEN

The salt spray suddenly turned to a heavy rain that lashed at Harriet's bare face and quickly soaked through her pants. A flash of lightning illuminated the Hog's empty parking spot, mocking them with the loss of their vehicle.

The rocks seemed to reverberate with the crack of thunder that followed. The thunder and lightning intensified until Harriet thought she was living in Shakespeare's *King Lear*.

Blow, winds, blow, and crack your cheeks! Rage! Blow!

She wished the storm would abate at least a little. She fumbled with the throat latch on her hood, trying to tighten it, but the wind ripped it from her stiff fingers. Cold rain plastered her hair to her head almost instantly and ran down the back of her neck.

Beside her, Mark was too full of recriminations to notice the storm. "Dammit. Why didn't I pocket the keys? I'm so used to leaving the resort carts and not thinking about it."

Another jagged bolt of lightning lit his dark figure as he

turned toward her. "I'm sorry. I've really screwed the pooch, haven't I?"

Harriet shook her head. She had to shout over the thunder that followed. "It's not your fault. Let's get inside and call Tarbell, let him know." She bent into the wind and led the way to the nearest cottage.

"Well, it's easy to see that someone's been staying here." Mark took off his jacket and hung it on a hook beside Harriet's. The cottage was a mess. Dirty dishes and empty drink containers were strewn around the living area, covering end tables and the floor.

"There's no cell reception," Harriet said. She shivered. Her wet clothes and hair felt icy in the cottage's cool interior. She tried to pull her pant legs away from her skin but they were plastered to her legs.

"We need to get out of these wet clothes. I'll see about getting some heat in here. Grab the blankets from the beds. You can undress in the bedroom while I look into the heat."

Harriet didn't argue. She shut the bedroom door behind her and stripped a blanket from one of the beds. She pulled down her pants but couldn't get them past her boots. "Oh for crying out loud, Harriet. Take off your boots you numbskull."

Off balance, she fell backward onto the bed. Her fingers felt cold and clumsy, making it difficult to untie her boot laces. She breathed a sigh of relief when she was finally able to pull them off. Her socks, pants, and underwear quickly followed. She hesitated over her tee shirts, then took them off as well but pulled her sweater back on even though it felt damp.

Folding a blanket in half, she wrapped it around her waist sarong-style. Holding it on with one hand she grabbed the other blanket, intending to head for the living area, but quickly realized she didn't have a free hand to open the door.

"You all right in there? I hate to report that there's no heat."

"Be right out!" She had a belt. That should work. She dropped the blanket and pulled the belt from her pants, wrapped the blanket around her waist again, and secured it with her belt.

"Here." She handed the other blanket to Mark. "I'm going to hang my clothes in the shower so they don't drip all over the floor." He took the blanket without a word and disappeared behind the second bedroom door.

The bathroom was as much of a mess as the living area. A sour smell rose from damp towels that had been tossed on the floor. A tube of toothpaste lay on the edge of the sink with its cap off and toothpaste oozing out onto the floor.

"Whoever is staying here is a slob," Harriet muttered. "The cleaners deserve every extra penny they're paid to clean up after guests like this."

Plucking a dirty tissue from the floor, she pushed it down on top of the overflowing wastebasket. A spot of blue appeared briefly, then disappeared beneath the mass of used tissues. Harriet hesitated. She really didn't want to dig through another person's dirty snot rags but curiosity won out. She upended the full waste container onto the floor. A caterpillar of blue hair tumbled out and lay at her feet.

"I'll be damned." Harriet left the mess on the floor and called Mark. When he poked his head in the bathroom door she pointed to the hair piece. "It's a wig. One of those bald wigs, only with a blue mohawk. It wasn't even Okido's real hair. You know what this means, don't you?"

Mark looked grim. "Yeah. It means Okido isn't really

missing; she must have had her disappearance planned out. I think we'd better move to another cottage. This could be a crime scene."

Harriet felt ill. They were no longer looking for a missing, possibly injured, woman. Okido could be a suspect in Alicia Wynn's murder. Had the producer been killed in the cottage and then dumped in the water on the island's west side?

She grabbed Mark's arm. "It was Okido who took the Hog. She could get away and we have no way to reach Tarbell to warn him."

"Unfortunately there's nothing we can do about any of it at the moment. Grab your things. We're headed next door."

Harriet dug up a trash bag to put their packs and wet clothes in and they headed to the neighboring cottage. Once there, they traded their newly soaked blankets for dry ones and spread the wet clothing and blankets around the cottage to dry.

"What a mess." Harriet sat in a cushioned chair with her knees up and the blanket wrapped firmly around her body. She was still shivering and she felt on edge and nervous. Okido had stolen the Hog and left them stranded. And the fact that she and Mark would be spending the night together was just beginning to sink in.

Mark looked at her with half-hooded eyes. He sat opposite her, his good foot resting on his left knee. His blanket had split open slightly, enough for her to see part of a well-muscled thigh. She blushed at the unexpected view and lowered her eyes.

She'd seen Mark in shorts, had seen his thighs before. It was stupid to feel embarrassed, but she was. She couldn't ignore the fact that he was probably naked under his blanket—just as she was.

"We should try to get back to the resort," she said. Could he hear the edge of panic in her voice?

"You want to walk through the jungle in the pouring rain at night. What about the jaguars and spiders and snakes? And can you imagine how muddy that road will be? We barely made it here in the Hog and that was before it began to rain." He shook his head. "No. Absolutely not. We stay put and call Tarbell in the morning after this storm clears out. He can send a boat for us."

Harriet groaned. Mark was right. Of course he was right. Only an insane or desperate person would try to to negotiate the interior road at night and in this weather. She wasn't insane. Was she feeling that desperate about being stuck overnight with Mark?

"I'm going to look for something to drink." She felt Mark's gaze burning into her back as she left the living area. She wasn't really thirsty, she just needed to put some space between her and Mark until she felt calmer.

How had she let herself get into this predicament? And what would Alex think when he learned that she and Mark had spent the night together? It didn't matter if they slept in separate rooms—*they were definitely sleeping in separate rooms*—they were still spending the night together with no one else around.

She stared sightlessly at the cabinet in front of her and pictured the man in the other room. Why, why, why hadn't she called Solly and asked him to help them search?

"Need a hand?"

Harriet jumped and whirled around. Mark stood a foot behind her, watching her with a puzzled expression. This close, she could see flecks of gold in his deep brown irises. How had she ever thought his eyes were cold? They were anything but. She felt the telltale heat from a blush climb her neck and spread across her cheeks.

"What's wrong?" He reached with a hand and gently brushed her wet hair back from her face. He rubbed her cheek with his thumb. "Talk to me."

She felt frozen, held in place by his thumb on her cheek and his gaze.

"It's nothing." Of course it was nothing. She was acting like a fifteen year old with her first crush. Just because Mark had called her beautiful and sensuous—it hadn't meant anything. It was probably his standard line. Of course—he said it to all the girls. Except that she wasn't only reacting to his words. She felt a yearning to touch him, to be held by him. To kiss him.

She jerked her gaze away from his mouth and made herself turn away and open cupboard doors.

"Ah. Just what the doctor ordered." Mark reached past her and pulled a half-full bottle of bourbon from the cabinet.

She hadn't even seen it. She really needed to get a grip if she was going to make it through the night. Mark was standing close enough for her to feel the heat radiating off his body. He smelled clean, like salt spray and rain and wind. She fought the urge to press against that heat and stepped to the side instead.

"This will warm us from the inside out. I prescribe a couple fingers of bourbon and a hot shower, then bed."

"I can't spend the night with you, Mark. It isn't right." She saw the skin around his eyes crinkle and his lips tighten and realized he was fighting a smile. A smile! She couldn't believe it—he found her discomfort humorous. She jabbed her finger into a chest that felt every bit as firm as it looked.

Focus, Harriet. Mark is the enemy.

"I'm involved with someone, in case you didn't know. I'm involved with Alex. Alex Hayes. We're going to get married once I get my head straightened out. So you see we can't spend the night together."

"All right. Would you feel better if I moved to another cottage?"

Harriet considered it for half a second. The rain was still coming down in sheets. It pounded on the cottage roof and sluiced down the windows. Only a hard-hearted bitch would send the man back into the storm.

"No. But we sleep in separate bedrooms."

"Fine. Now that our sleeping arrangements are settled, grab a couple glasses. I don't know about you but I could use a drink." He turned and left the kitchen, his blade tapping a slow beat on the wood floor.

Harriet found two clean glasses and followed Mark from the kitchen. He set the bottle on the side table next to his chair and plopped down with a heavy sigh. She set the glasses next to it, waited for him to pour and hand her one, and headed back to the safety of her chair.

"What shall we drink to?" Mark asked. His gaze was steady on her face. "I know. Let's drink to the storm ending soon, Okido being caught . . . and to new friends. We *can* be friends, can't we? Even if you are *involved* with Alex?"

"Don't be snide. Of course we can be friends." She raised her glass. "To the end of the storm, Okido's capture, and new friends." She took a long swallow of the bourbon and gasped as the fire spread through her chest and body.

"Holy moon rocks!"

Mark grinned at her. "Bourbon is meant to be more of a sipping drink, not a thirst quencher. Is it warming you up?"

Harriet could only nod and blink back the tears in her eyes. She waited for the flames to die down before braving another–more cautious–sip. Her skin felt flushed and the cottage no longer felt chilly. This was a good thing. She drank more, loving the soft, fuzzy glow the bourbon put on everything.

"I definitely feel warmer. This was a good idea."

A dimple appeared in Mark's right cheek. He had a nice smile. She smiled back.

"What did you mean when you said you were going to get married once you get your head straightened out? Are you opposed to marriage?"

Harriet took another sip. She liked the way the bourbon made her breathe fire. She wondered if she could light her breath with a match. Just like a dragon. How cool would that be?

"Harriet? What's wrong with your head? I want to understand."

She wagged the head in question from side to side. "My head is broken. My aunt took me to a doctor when I was eight and he broke it. Payson's friend Dr. Bainbridge is going to try to put it back together again. Just like Humpty Dumpty." She giggled, then grew sad.

"Only all the king's horses and all the king's men couldn't put Humpty together again, could they? I'm not sure my head can be fixed either."

Mark frowned. He reached over and half-filled Harriet's glass and added more to his own, then sipped his drink while he tried to make sense of Harriet's words.

"Your aunt took you to see a shrink? How did he break your head?" He winced when Harriet drained her glass. She was going to feel the booze in the morning and not in a good way.

"Alex won't marry me until I know. He has the pieces. Payson has the pieces. They won't tell me. 'Snot fair." She closed her eyes. Her voice thickened. "Can't talk about it.

Too much pain. Too much pain." Her chin dropped to her chest.

Mark grabbed the glass from Harriet's fingers before she dropped it. "I do believe you're drunk, sweetheart. Come on, let's get you to bed so you don't wake up with a crick in your neck."

He set her glass on the floor and slid one arm under Harriet's knees and the other under her back. Bracing himself, he lifted her against his chest. Her head lolled against his shoulder. Her hair smelled of jasmine and citrus mixed with salt spray. He let himself hold her for several minutes, smelling her and enjoying the feel of her lean, muscled body against his.

He took her into the bedroom that still had blankets on the beds and laid her on one until he could pull back the bedding on the other one. Briefly, he debated removing her blanket for comfort's sake, but decided against it. He had a feeling that Harriet would be embarrassed if she woke up naked beneath the sheets. He transferred her to the prepared bed and covered her.

"Don't go," she mumbled.

Mark stopped at the door and turned. "What?"

"Don't go," she murmured. "I'm cold and I don't want to be alone. Hold me."

He hesitated. He had intended to sleep in the other bedroom. Sleeping in the other bedroom was the right thing to do.

"Please."

The plea broke down his resolve to do the right thing. "Be right back." Mark turned out the lights in the cottage and returned to the bedroom, feeling his way carefully in the dark. He tried to slip into the bed with his blanket wrapped around him but it came loose and fell to the floor.

He stood again and looked down at the bed. It would really be best if he slept in the other room.

"Mark? Don't make me sleep alone. I want you to hold me."

What could he do? She had said please and there was a limit to his virtuousness. Mark slid under the sheets. There wasn't much room for two adults in the twin bed. Harriet was facing the wall. He wrapped his arm around her and pulled her snug against his chest, careful to keep his blade away from her feet. He should have removed it but being one-footed would put him at a disadvantage if Okido came back.

Harriet fell asleep immediately, snoring softly.

Not wanting to miss a single moment, Mark lay awake for what felt like hours.

CHAPTER SIXTEEN

The first thing Harriet noticed when she woke the following morning was the wall two feet from her face.

This was not her bedroom.

She rolled onto her back and squinted at the bright sunlight streaming through the room's only window. The storm must have blown itself out while she slept.

The bright light hurt her eyes and stabbed at her brain, not unlike the sharp pain she experienced whenever she tried to retrieve her memories. She buried her face in the pillow and groaned at the dull ache the movement brought on. After several minutes she opened her eyes again, holding her hand to shade them.

What had she done to herself? Her tongue felt thick and dry and her mouth tasted sour. She thought back to the previous evening. Sitting in the living area with Mark.

Bourbon.

Mark had found a bottle of bourbon. She couldn't handle hard liquor–had never been able to–but she'd conveniently forgotten that little fact because she'd been worried about spending the night with Mark.

She had behaved like an immature teen instead of a mature woman. She had gulped down several glasses of the foul-tasting stuff until her vision blurred and she had passed out. How embarrassing.

Once she and Solly had stolen a bottle of tequila they found in an unlocked car. Solly had gleefully challenged her to see who could hold their liquor better and they had emptied the bottle shot by shot. Solly passed out on the floor of their one room studio apartment. She had declared herself winner and left the apartment. She woke up in the neighborhood park the next day, stiff and sore and hungover, and swore never to drink again.

Apparently it was a lesson that needed to be repeated.

The enticing smell of coffee penetrated her thoughts. That meant Mark was up and about. More memories came flooding back. Had she really begged Mark to sleep with her? How was she ever going to live that down? And how was she going to explain her actions to Alex?

Maybe she wouldn't have to. Maybe she could convince Mark to keep it a secret, a one-off, one that would never be repeated.

"I am such an idiot." She swung her legs over the side of the bed and sat up with a moan. At least she was still wearing her sweater and blanket.

"Don't be a coward, Harriet. Go out there and act as if nothing happened." She rewrapped and secured her blanket and stepped out of the bedroom. There was no sign of Mark in the living area. His clothes were no longer draped over the furniture and a blanket was folded neatly on a chair. Squaring her shoulders, she walked into the kitchen with a smile on her face.

The kitchen was also empty. A clean mug sat next to the half-full coffee pot along with two aspirin. A thoughtful gesture on Mark's part. Grateful for the reprieve, Harriet poured herself some hot coffee and gulped the bitter, nutty brew. She pulled a water from the chiller and swallowed the aspirin. The day immediately began to look better.

Draining her coffee, she refilled the mug and went in search of her clothes. While not soaking wet, they were still damp and difficult to pull on. She skipped her socks and wet boots and stepped out of the cottage. Now that she felt more human she wondered where Mark had gone off to.

"Mark? Mark!"

The rocks in front of the cottage felt gritty and cold on her feet, but the sun's rays felt wonderful on her face. She closed her eyes and stood for several minutes to let it warm her body and clothing while she sipped her second cup of coffee.

Her thoughts eventually turned to the discovery she'd made in the next cottage. She needed to find Mark so they could figure out what they should do about Okido, if anything. It was time to get moving.

She stepped back inside the cottage, rinsed out the coffee pot and her mug, and set them on the dish towel next to the sink which already held a clean mug and the two bourbon glasses. Even though the mug and glasses were already dry—which meant they'd been there a while—she didn't think that Mark would venture far and leave her alone.

Harriet grimaced as she pulled on her cold wet socks and boots and hoped her feet would warm up once she got moving. The day was warming fast and the extra layers she wore felt unnecessary. She peeled off the sweater and her long-sleeved tee, stuffed them into her pack, and stepped outside again.

Unlike the previous day, the ocean positively sparkled

with a billion tiny mirrors that pierced her brain like flashing miniature knives stabbing at the inside of her head. She hurried back inside the cottage and hunted up her canvas pack and her sunglasses.

"Much better." The headache was rapidly receding.

Where had Mark gone off to? A quick scan to the left and the right revealed the cottages evenly spaced on a curved line along the exposed, rocky shore–but no sign of Mark. She couldn't see the beach from where she stood, but there were three sets of metal stairs leading down, a stairway for every four cottages. She saw floats at the far end of each stairway for the boats that the guests and housekeepers used to travel from one side of the island to the other.

Perhaps Mark had gone to check on the condition of the boat Okido had used to get there, looking to see if they could use it to return to the main resort once the seas died down and became navigable again.

She headed over the rocks to the nearest set of stairs to her right. They hadn't bothered to search the rest of the cottages. According to Tarbell there was only one female guest staying in the east cottages. She assumed that guest had been Okido.

What if Okido had broken into the cottage and there was another guest staying in one of the cottages they hadn't searched, a guest who had seen Okido? Would Okido hurt the guest to keep them from reporting her presence?

She had to check the rest of the cottages.

It took thirty minutes to walk through the remaining six cottages, thirty wasted minutes since they were all empty. Rather than walk back to the middle set of stairs, Harriet took the last set down to its float. A pair of wheels attached to the underside of the last step allowed the metal stairs to roll and raise and lower as the floats moved up and down with the tide.

Because it was close to high tide the stairs extended well onto the floats. Looking back at the shore, she saw that the only way onto the beach was to climb down the rocks. The narrow strip of sand was littered with brown mounds of thick, tubular seaweed and dark driftwood tossed up by the storm.

Harriet walked back up the stairs and over the rocks to the center set of stairs. There was only one boat in sight, tied up to the center float. It bumped rhythmically against the float with each wave that slapped against its side. The boat had received some damage in the storm from banging against the float, but she was glad to see that the damage was nothing that made it unusable. The paint was scraped and the port gunwale had been crushed in a couple spots. Nothing Leonard's drones couldn't easily fix.

She jumped aboard and tossed the bumpers out to protect the side from further damage. The cabin door was locked. Sliding onto the helm seat, she lifted the cover that protected the controls and was surprised to find the boat key in the ignition. She tried the bilge pumps and emptied the rainwater sloshing around the deck.

Had Okido tried to use the boat the previous day and then aborted when she realized the water was too rough for small craft? She must have thought it was her lucky day when they had arrived in the Hog.

Harriet pocketed the key and headed back up the stairs. At least with the boat they had a way back to the main resort once the seas calmed a bit more.

She hugged the right side of the stairs and searched the beach for any sign of Mark. She was beginning to feel uneasy. They should have bumped into each other by now. Because she was looking off to her right, she almost missed the boot in the shadows beneath the stairs. She caught it from the corner of her eye, something that looked out of place and therefore drew her attention.

She climbed through the rail and carefully slid and jumped her way down to the skinny band of fine white sand. Clouds of disturbed sand flies surrounded her as she skirted the seaweed and tried to avoid the driftwood and the waves lapping near her feet.

"Mark!" Mark's body lay beneath the stairs next to the rocks. Dressed in dark clothing and lying in the stairway's shadow like he was, she was lucky she hadn't missed him.

"Mark, can you hear me?"

There was no movement and no response to her question. Harriet's heart thudded in her chest. What could have happened? She knelt in the sand and gently felt Mark's neck for a pulse. It was thready but beating–he wasn't dead. Relieved but puzzled, she sat back on her heels. Had he slipped and fallen from the rocks?

Impossible. He wouldn't be under the stairs if that was the case–unless he had crawled there.

She was about to roll him onto his back when she noticed two things almost simultaneously; there was something dark and wet looking in his hair on the back of his head, and his blade was missing. His pant leg was pushed up above his stump. She winced at the sight of angry red scar tissue.

If his prosthetic had fallen off it should still be nearby. She searched the beach and rocks near Mark's body but didn't see it.

There was only one explanation: Mark had been taken by surprise and attacked from behind. Okido must have returned.

It didn't take long for her to find the weapon. A rock smeared with blood lay in the sand not far from Mark. She found the suspension sleeve for his blade tossed on a mound of seaweed but no sign of the blade itself.

When she'd first seen his prosthetic she'd been curious and looked them up. She learned that if an amputee used a suspension sleeve there should also be a silicone sleeve worn over his stump and several pair of thick socks. She searched for another few minutes but couldn't find anything more.

Harriet returned to Mark, dropped to her knees, and gently gripped his shoulder. She didn't dare roll him onto his back, afraid that could do more damage to his skull.

Waves lapped perilously close to Mark's body. She knew she didn't have the strength necessary to carry him up the rocks and he was already lying right up against their base. If the tide came in much farther she'd have to think of something.

"Mark. Can you hear me?" When he didn't answer she picked up his hand and chafed it between her own. It felt cold and limp and frightened her. Head injuries were one of the most common causes of disability and death in adults. She didn't know the first thing about what first aid she should be doing. What if he had swelling in the brain? Or bone fragments? Mark needed a doctor asap. She took off her pack and dug out her link.

"Oh, thank god," she said when she heard Tarbell's voice. She told him everything that had happened since finding Okido's mohawk wig. "I don't know how to help him. What do I do? The tide's coming in and he hasn't moved and he's not responding to my voice."

"Stay with him. I'm going to call Dr. Clarke. She and Alex are on their way back to the island. I'll see if I can get one of our pilots to ferry her over to you in the small chopper. If not I'll have her call you. I'm pretty busy here so I can't come myself."

"What happened? Is anyone hurt?"

"Nothing serious. I'm at the marina with Leonard. The teens who found Alicia Wynn thought it would be fun to snag the jetskis and jump the storm swells. They got a bit more of a ride than they bargained for. They're shaken up but okay. I'm mostly dealing with damage control and handling hot parents and a few guests who think the resort should be able to control the weather."

Harriet heard someone call for Fox. "Gotta skedaddle, Harry. I'll call Dr. Clarke right now."

"Thanks, Tarbell." Harriet put her link in her pocket in case she needed to get to it quick. Pulling her pack back on, she sank to her knees next to Mark. She picked up his hand again and pressed it to her chest between her breasts, hoping to transfer some warmth to him. She'd read somewhere that recovered coma patients often reported being able to hear when others talked to them.

She cast around for something to say. "Help is on the way." She looked down at Mark's pale face, the strong, hooked nose, his full mouth.

"You can be a frustrating man, you know. You've shaken me up and you confuse me and I don't like it one little bit. I don't just mean this." She flapped her free hand at his body. "Although having a bashed skull is pretty damn disturbing." She hesitated.

"I despised you when we first met. You looked at me through those dark eyes of yours and I knew you found me lacking. And your snide remarks put me on the defensive. It was obvious you didn't think much of me and that hit all my insecurity buttons."

Harriet reached down and brushed the hair back from Mark's forehead. His skin felt cold and clammy. She wished she dared to move him into the sunlight but she was afraid to do anything until she heard from the doctor.

"When you helped me and Solly search for Okido I began to see another side of you. You became . . . more human. Less of a rigid calculating machine. And then you had to go and say all those nice things about me. Why'd you do that? I *hate* that I'm attracted to you, dammit. Do you hear me? What kind of woman is attracted to two different men? A woman of loose morals, that's what kind. I love Alex, I really do, but–and I'm going to be brutally honest here–I'm attracted to you."

"Sorry." The word was spoken so softly Harriet thought she might have imagined it.

"Mark?" Harriet leaned close to his face but there was no response.

Harriet's link rang. She pulled it from her pocket, hoping that it was Dr. Clarke and not Tarbell informing her that it was still too windy to fly the chopper.

"Harriet? Are you all right?"

"Alex? I'm fine, but Mark is unconscious. Is Dr. Clarke with you?"

"We're five minutes out from the island. Tarbell has the chopper standing by. We should be there in less than fifteen. Harriet, how did Mark get hurt?"

"I-I'm not sure. It looks as if someone hit him on the back of the head with a rock." There was silence on the other end of the call.

"I want you to get inside one of the cottages and lock yourself in until I get there."

Harriet looked down at Mark's still body. "I can't do that, Alex. I can't leave Mark unprotected. Just get here as soon as you can." She ended the call and put her link away. She looked up and down the beach but saw no one. Was Okido hiding in the shadows under one of the other stairways? Or watching from the rocks above?

Unfortunately the rocks were too high for Harriet to see over them from where she sat.

It had to be Okido who attacked Mark–there was no one else on the east side of the island. The chances that she'd been able to drive the Hog over the interior road in the storm in the dark had been slim to none. She must have gotten stuck, hiked back to the cottages, and surprised Mark on the rocks.

She would have come back for the boat. Why didn't she take it after she attacked Mark?

"I won't be far. Don't run away." Harriet climbed the rocks and scanned the cove. She needed a spot where she could watch for anyone approaching and also see Mark. It became immediately clear that the rocks wouldn't do. She couldn't see Mark from the top. She'd have to watch from the stairs.

The tide was almost full and the stairs had leveled out even more. She walked partway out the stairway and leaned sideways against the right rail. She could see the entire beach and across the rocks and the front of all twelve cottages, but she could only see Mark's foot and it made her nervous.

What if he regained consciousness and panicked? What if the tide covered his head and he drowned while she was watching from the stairway?

She ran back to the rocks and climbed back down to the beach and under the stairway. This time when she knelt next to Mark pools of water gathered around her knees and waves lapped at her lower legs. Without the sun to warm her the water felt cold.

What she needed was a dyke to hold back the water. She began heaping wet sand into a long, snakelike mound around Mark's body. She had nearly finished when she heard a thud behind her.

"What did you do with the boat key?"

Harriet froze, then slowly swiveled her head to look at the woman standing less than five feet away. Dressed in matching black with white swirls lycra shorts and bra top, the woman's strong body, with muscular arms and thighs and very little body fat, left little doubt as to her identity.

It took Harriet a moment to register the weapon in Okido's right hand. She recognized the knife as coming from one of the sets she'd seen in each of the cottage kitchens; a long, slim-bladed filet knife used for boning fish. It was sharp and sturdy and very capable of doing serious damage to a human body.

"You-" She swallowed and tried to find her voice. "You must be Okido." The stuntwoman-turned-personal-assistant looked older than Harriet had expected, although that could be partly blamed on the fine lines bracketing her mouth and the bruised, pouchy skin under her eyes–a clear sign of sleepless nights.

Quick as lightning, the woman lashed out. Harriet felt a sharp sting on her bicep. She jerked back and pressed her hand over the wound.

"I said, where's the bloody boat key? Answer me quick or it'll be your friend next."

CHAPTER SEVENTEEN

Harriet never took her eyes off the knife in Okido's hand as she stood slowly. Her attempt to dam the advancing tide from Mark was working, at least temporarily. It wouldn't hold for long, but it didn't need to; judging by the narrow strip of dry sand at the base of the rocks, the cove was at full tide and soon the water would begin to ebb.

It worried her that Okido looked a little crazed—worried but didn't surprise her. Even in the shadows beneath the stairway, Harriet could see that Okido's eyes were bloodshot from lack of sleep. They held anger and desperation—never a good combination.

Worse, she was armed and obviously skilled with a knife. Harriet wouldn't have been surprised to learn that Okido had stunt-doubled for a knife-wielding crazy woman in one of her films.

The knife wound on her arm burned. She felt something warm and wet running through her fingers but she resisted looking at it. She didn't want to know how badly she'd been cut, but more than that, she was afraid to take her gaze off the woman in front of her.

Okido waved the knife in a menacing manner and held out her free hand. "Boat key or your friend dies. Now!"

The low whump-whump of a chopper approaching from the west penetrated Harriet's awareness. Help was on its way. All she had to do was keep Okido from killing Mark.

Easy enough. Give Okido the key and let her leave. She let go of her wounded arm and reached into her pocket, pulled out the boat key, and held it out to Okido. Blood dripped off her elbow and plopped into the water where it swirled and spread in a pale pink cloud.

"Here, take the key. Just out of curiosity, how did you know I had it?"

"Toss it here."

Harriet threw the key into the water at Okido's feet. Okido fished it up with a bare foot and snatched the key from the air. Despite her fear, Harriet couldn't help but be impressed by the woman's athleticism. Every move she made looked controlled and fluid.

"I slept on the boat last night after you and your friend showed up," Okido said. "I heard you climb aboard the boat this morning."

The cabin door had been locked when Harriet checked. After she found the key she didn't think to unlock it. Now she was glad she hadn't bothered to search the cabin. She felt sure that Okido would have killed her if Harriet had found her hiding in the boat.

"Why did you disappear? Alicia was worried about you. She even accused her husband of banishing you from the island."

"That was part of the plan. I disappear, Haywood gets blamed. Alicia staged that argument so others would hear."

Small waves lapped at Harriet's ankles, sucking away

the sand beneath her feet. Her boots were soaked through and her jeans wet to her knees. She shivered.

"I don't understand." Harriet frowned. She took a sideways step to place herself more between Mark and Okido. She needed to buy time until Alex arrived in the chopper. She risked a glance at Mark. Was his color worse?

"Why would Alicia want to get her husband in trouble?"

"She wasn't happy with Dirk. He was a mistake." Two bright red spots appeared on Okido's pale cheeks. "Alicia and me—we'd been lovers years ago, when Li first got started producing films. Then she signed on Dirk for her first action film. He swept her off her feet and they got married. I couldn't believe it. Hollywood's glamour couple. What a sham." Okido's voice shook with disgust.

"It couldn't last, of course. Li loved *me,* not him. She got me the job as Haywood's PA so we could be together more without anyone getting suspicious. Haywood was supposed to die while we were here at the resort but Li changed her mind about everything."

"Alicia's husband was supposed to die at the resort?" How had the resort become the go-to destination for murders? Harriet narrowed her eyes at Okido. "Just how did you plan to kill off Mr. Haywood? This sounds like the stupidest plan ever. First you disappear, then Dirk Haywood dies? That leaves Alicia Wynn holding the proverbial bag."

"No, we had a good plan. Dirk was going to be blamed for my disappearance. We were going to make it look like he took his own life—in remorse—you know? Li staged arguments with him to make him look angry and unstable. I was going to hit her, produce a few bruises, and she'd say Dirk hit her. Then he would die and Li would put it about that Dirk couldn't deal with the bad publicity so he offed himself. It was a good plan," she repeated.

"How did you plan to get off the island after you killed Dirk?"

"Easy. People only notice a person's dominate feature. Everyone will be looking for a woman with a blue mohawk." She shrugged. "I'll leave as a blonde. You only photograph arrivals; the head count would match so no one would even notice me."

Harriet shook her head. Could the woman be this stupid? "The head count would be off by one, Okido. You're supposed to be missing, remember? Something went wrong, didn't it? *You* killed Alicia. Why?"

A red flush crept up Okido's neck and face. Harriet couldn't tell if the woman was growing angrier or more upset or both. She tried to gentle her voice. "Why did you kill Alicia, Okido? I want to understand."

"I didn't kill her. I admit, I was pissed; Li ruined everything. She wanted to toss out all the plans we had worked on for years. We were supposed to get married, but then she changed her mind."

Okido's eyes filled with tears. "*We had a plan.* I picked Li up in the boat and brought her here to work out the last of the details for Haywood's fake suicide. She was acting distant. When I asked her what was wrong she told me she couldn't be seen with me after Dirk died–that it would look too suspicious. We argued. I swear she was still alive when I dropped her on the beach below the resort."

The sound of the chopper grew closer. Okido stepped out from beneath the stairs and narrowed her eyes at the sky.

"Change in plans," she said. "You're coming with me. I might need a hostage to bargain with. Get up those rocks and walk down to the boat. As long as you do as I say your friend will live."

"How do I know you won't kill him even if I do as you say?"

Okido grinned. "You don't. But I'll kill him for sure if you *don't* do as I tell you. And then I'll kill you. I'm feeling just desperate enough to do it."

Harriet scrambled up the rocks and walked down the stairway to the float. Okido joined her a minute later. She pointed the blade at Harriet's stomach. Now that they were out of the stairway's shadow the blade glinted in the sun and looked even more lethal. Harriet couldn't take her eyes off it.

"In the boat. Do exactly as I tell you."

Harriet forced herself to look away from the knife and step into the boat. Okido unknotted the line from one of the bumpers and tied Harriet's hands behind her back, then pushed Harriet to the deck.

"Sit. And don't move unless I tell you." She started the engines, untied the bow and stern lines, and eased away from the float. Once clear, she turned the boat in a wide arc away from shore and gunned the engines. The stern dropped as the bow lifted above the waves. Water sprayed from the sides and the hull began to slam hard, up and down against the rough chop.

Without the use of her hands to steady herself, Harriet slid back to the stern when Okido hit the throttle. She stretched her legs out and wedged her body across the transom to keep from getting tossed over the twin engines and into their propellers.

Cold wet spray soaked through her still damp clothes and she was soon shivering. She jerked her hands in an effort to loosen the knots but Okido had tied them too tightly together for her to get any kind of play in the rope.

A shadow passed over the boat. Harriet looked up and saw Alex sitting next to the chopper pilot. He looked grim.

"Looks like the cavalry has arrived!" shouted Okido. She left the helm and worked her way back to the stern. Squatting down next to Harriet, she suddenly smiled.

Harriet didn't like the looks of that smile. "What are you going to do?"

"Just this." Okido picked Harriet up and tossed her over the back of the boat.

Harriet barely had time to take a breath before the water closed over her head. The whine of the propellers faded and her world turned silent. She fought the panic that she knew would kill her if she didn't beat it. She knew how to swim and loved the water. She just needed to think clearly and figure out how to survive.

Time slowed. The saltwater made her wounded arm sting. She heard the muted whump of the chopper blades, almost in time with her heartbeat.

Staying afloat without the use of her hands was difficult. Floating while fully dressed and wearing boots proved to be impossible. Even her full canvas pack added to the problem. Once it, her sweater, long-sleeved tee, and jacket became waterlogged, they increased the weight she had to fight against.

She forced herself to relax her body to see if it would float to the surface, but too many things were dragging her down. Something hit the water nearby. She twisted and tried to see but the usually clear water was still murky from the storm. The faint, long dark shape could be any number of things.

She'd read stories about dolphins helping drowning swimmers and believed in the possibility, but those swimmers had their hands free to grab onto the dolphin. She was going to have to save herself.

Kicking her feet as hard as she could, she felt encouraged when she rose a few feet, but she soon tired and her kicks grew feeble.

She was running out of air. Sparkling dots of light began to appear at the edge of her vision. Unable to stop herself, she released some of the stale air she was holding in her lungs. Soon her lungs would force her to breathe in and then the struggle would be done with. She wondered if her parents would be there to greet her.

Something grabbed her by her pack and began to drag her. Shark. She was bleeding. The blood must have attracted it. She knew that sharks could smell the minutest amount of blood from great distances.

She had to fight it. She squirmed and kicked out to no avail. She was still being dragged. It took her a minute to realize she was being dragged up toward the sunlight–to the surface.

Maybe Okido had had second thoughts and had come back to fish her out. She felt legs kick against her own and renewed her own efforts to help but she had nothing left to give. Her chest ached from holding her breath. She released the remainder of her air.

She felt bad for whoever was helping her because she knew that she wasn't going to make it. They were rescuing a dead woman.

They broke the surface just as Harriet started to suck in a lungful of water. She coughed hard and took in several huge, gulping sobs of life-giving oxygen and tried to twist to see who had saved her.

"I've got you," said a voice in her ear.

"Alex!" A stuttering sob escaped, then another. "How-how did you find me so fast?"

"Amos got me near where you went in and I jumped."

"I was drowning. I've never been so scared." She couldn't help it, she began to cry.

"Shh. Don't cry. We're not out of this yet. We have to swim to the life rings Dr. Clarke tossed for us. They aren't far. Think you can make it?"

Panic seized Harriet. "Don't let go of me. Okido tied my hands. I can't swim without my hands."

She felt Alex treading water behind her. "This is what we'll do. Roll onto your back. I'll get us both to the rings. Like I said, they aren't far. I can free your hands once we have something to hold you up."

Once her hands were free, Harriet was able to hang onto the ring and kick for shore. They weren't as far out as she had feared; Okido had still been well inside the mouth of the cove when she tossed Harriet overboard.

By the time they made the beach, Dr. Eleanor Clarke and the pilot were waiting for them on the rocks. Eleanor had her medic bag with her and the pilot carried a narrow stretcher. Harriet dropped to her knees.

"Where's the man with the head wound?" called Dr. Clarke. "I don't see anyone."

"You have to come down here." Harriet forced herself to her feet and pointed to the middle stairs. "He's under those stairs."

It took Alex, the pilot, Dr. Clarke, and Harriet to maneuver the stretcher up the rocks with Mark's inert body strapped to it. Dr. Clarke looked grim when she examined Mark's head injury. She called the hospital on the mainland and asked them to set up an operating room and find a surgeon with head trauma experience.

"Will he be all right?" Harriet asked.

"I don't know. I won't know the extent of the injury to his brain until they can take x-rays, but the fact that he's been unconscious since you found him concerns me. The head trauma specialist will meet us at the hospital."

Harriet remembered Mark's "sorry."

"I think he was partly conscious when I first found him. He said one word, but that was it."

There wasn't room in the chopper for all of them, especially with Mark laid out on the stretcher. Dr. Clarke insisted that Harriet accompany them to the hospital so she could clean and stitch up the knife wound in her arm.

Harriet hesitated before climbing into the waiting chopper. "Alex, thank you." She kissed his cheek. "I'll get back to the island as quickly as I can."

Alex hugged her tight to his chest and buried his face in her hair. "You have to stop putting yourself in danger. I can't handle the thought of losing you. If Amos hadn't seen what was happening and flown close enough for me to reach you . . ."

"But he did. Thanks to you and Amos I didn't drown. You rescued me. Get in touch with Solly and let him know I'm okay, will you please?"

"Harriet. We have to go now." Amos gestured for her to get in the chopper.

"I have to go." Harriet climbed into the chopper and strapped in. She watched Alex get smaller and smaller and finally disappear from sight. Behind her, Mark lay silent, his skin gray, his breathing barely discernible.

She took his cold hand, closed her eyes, and prayed for Mark to recover while Dr. Clarke wrapped a gauze bandage around her arm to stop the bleeding.

"You're definitely going to need stitches. You've lost quite a bit of blood."

She felt woozy and exhausted from her ordeal. An image of her aunt came to her, dressed in her Sunday best. Aunt Wendy had insisted that Harriet attend their church every Sunday even though Harriet told her she didn't believe in God. And yet when she was at her most distressed or frightened, Harriet found herself turning to

God in prayer. Perhaps she believed in a higher power after all.

"We have to switch to a shuttle." The pilot's voice in her headphones startled Harriet. She must have fallen asleep almost as soon as she closed her eyes. She turned quickly to check on Mark but he looked no different, still gray and clammy. His chest barely moved with his breath.

"I don't understand," she said, facing the pilot again. "Isn't time of the essence? We have to get Mark to the hospital."

"Even if this chopper could make it to the mainland on the amount of fuel we have and with a full load, the shuttles are five times faster. I called ahead–they have a shuttle waiting to take off as soon as we transfer your friend."

Even though it only took fifteen minutes, every second of the journey to the shuttle field felt like an eternity. At last they landed. The chopper was immediately surrounded by people and droids; Mark was carefully unloaded and placed in Payson's personal shuttle. Harriet found Payson waiting for her when she boarded.

Unlike the other trips she'd taken with Payson when he wore one of his business suits, he was dressed in khakis and a white, loose, long-sleeved tunic and sandals. Seeing Payson in casual dress drove home the seriousness of Mark's situation. If Payson hadn't taken the time to put on a business suit he had to be worried.

"Payson." Harriet's voice wobbled. She collapsed in the seat next to Payson and closed her eyes. "He's in a bad way. Why does shit like this happen to good people?"

Payson took her hand between his and rubbed it gently. "Mark is strong. He'll pull through. I have two neurosurgeons waiting for our arrival." He eyed the bloody bandage on her arm. "You've been hurt."

Harriet glanced at the bandage. She had nearly

forgotten it was there, but realized the cut was throbbing. "It's nothing."

"Solly packed a bag for you with dry clothes. Why don't you go back to the bathroom and take a hot shower and change? We could be in for a long wait at the hospital. You'll feel more comfortable in dry clothes."

Harriet hadn't even considered that she was sitting on Payson's leather seats in wet clothes. She sprang to her feet. "I'm so sorry. I forgot I was wet."

"Harriet." Payson's voice was firm. "I don't care about the blasted seat. It can be replaced. I care about you. Take a hot shower, change into dry clothes, and I'll see about getting you something to eat."

"No, no food. I couldn't eat anything. I'm all tied up in knots."

"Maybe just a cup of hot tea then. Your clothes are in the bathroom."

Harriet nodded and made her way to the rear of the shuttle.

CHAPTER EIGHTEEN

If Harriet thought the chopper ride across the island took forever, then the shuttle trip to the mainland hospital took an eternity. The hot shower and the dry clothes Solly had packed for her felt heavenly. She sipped at hot tea while she told Payson everything that had happened–leaving out the fact that she and Mark had spent the previous night in the same bed.

She still felt conflicting emotions about her attraction to Mark. She knew asking him to sleep with her had been poorly done of her, even if all they did was sleep. If she hadn't been drunk and ready to pass out could she say the same thing? Or would she have wanted more?

The fact that she couldn't answer that question with a firm no tied her up in knots. She wished she could talk to Solly; Solly would help her work out what she was feeling. They had been each other's sounding boards almost from the day they'd met. One runaway teen helping another. No one knew her as well as Solomon Ayers; sometimes she thought he knew her better than she did herself. What would he say about her attraction to Mark?

Payson said very little during the flight. She had the distinct impression that he was preoccupied, and once she'd told him everything she intended to share she fell quiet, closing her eyes so he wouldn't feel obliged to make small talk.

Mark was whisked away as soon as they landed in the hospital's shuttle lot. Once Harriet's knife wound had been cleaned, stitched, and bandaged, Payson arranged two private rooms for them on the top floor of the hospital's guest wing. They waited together in Harriet's room while the doctors assessed Mark's condition and then whisked him into surgery.

"Shouldn't we be waiting in the OR's waiting room?" Harriet asked. She felt antsy, unable to sit for more than a few seconds before she sprang up to pace again.

"They know where we are," Payson assured her. "As soon as there is news, we'll hear." He had a pizza delivered to the room along with a bottle of white wine, hoping to pique Harriet's appetite.

She tried a bite, but the pizza—one of her favorite foods—tasted like clay in her mouth. She forced herself to chew and swallow the bite then set the slice down. "Thanks, Payson, but I don't think I can eat right now."

Payson stood at the window, looking out at the green courtyard that separated the hospitality wing from the main hospital. "I know how you feel. Let's get out of here," he said over his shoulder. "The surgery will take at least eight hours. There won't be any news until then. I'll go nuts sitting around for all that time."

"But if something happens while Mark is on the table—" *If he dies and we're not here,* she wanted to say. If Mark died she'd forever feel bad that she wasn't available even if there was nothing she could do to prevent it. The thought of Mark dying left a hollow feeling in her chest. He didn't deserve to die–not now, not like this. Not after recently surviving a bomb that was meant to kill him.

Payson took Harriet's arm and steered her toward the door. "Eleanor will let us know if anything happens. If she calls we'll come right back. I've arranged a private room for Mark once he's out of the ICU. Easy to access and you can see his window from here."

Harriet insisted on inspecting Mark's room before they left. It was a large single, bright and airy with a massive flat screen tv on the wall opposite the bed. The windows opened to let in the fresh air. The floor was quiet, the nurse's station set in the tee intersection at the far end of the hall. She wished they were closer but knew Payson would make sure Mark was closely monitored.

She would bring flowers back with her for the room, something bright and cheerful to look at when he opened his eyes. "Before we go, could you call Eleanor and tell her to contact us if his condition changes even the slightest bit?"

If Payson wondered why she was so concerned about Mark, he didn't let on. After he made the call they rode the lift down to the ground floor in silence and walked toward the exit. The street level corridors and lobby were packed with visitors speaking in hushed tones and multiple languages.

People passed them with worried, hollowed out expressions on their faces; no doubt heading to see sick loved ones. Others looked joyful. Many hobbled past with canes and walkers, a few pushed in wheelchairs. The place smelled of antiseptic and fear and too many varieties of perfume. It made Harriet long for the tranquility and fresh air of the island.

She wondered briefly about the destination Payson had in mind, but she didn't care enough to ask. Anything that would help the next eight hours pass quickly would be a welcome distraction.

They stepped outside the hospital into bright Florida sunshine. Harriet fumbled in her pack and pulled out her shades. "Where are we going?"

A black limo pulled in front of the building. The driver, dressed in a slim, dark blue skirt and and jacket, got out and approached them. "Mr. Douglas? My name is Jonelle. I'll be your driver this afternoon." She opened the rear door and stood aside.

Harriet climbed into the car, thankful that it wasn't a stretch limo. She would have felt wrong riding around in luxury while Mark fought for his life somewhere in the building behind them. She glanced at Payson beside her. Other than a tightness around his pale blue eyes, he looked perfectly relaxed. He probably used hired cars and drivers whenever he traveled. For him a limo would be a normal mode of transportation.

Payson gave the driver an address that sounded familiar to Harriet, but again, she didn't care enough to pursue it. It wasn't until they stopped in front of the steel and glass building set on a canal that Harriet realized why the address sounded familiar.

"Why are we here?" A knot of panic rose in Harriet's chest. "I don't want to deal with Dr. Bainbridge today. Let's go back to the hospital."

"Ed has some news for us. I thought we might as well get it in person since we're in town." He released his safety belt and waited for Jonelle to open his door.

When Jonelle came around to open Harriet's door, she sat there staring at the building. "I really, *really* don't want to go in there."

Payson leaned into the open door and held out his

hand. "You have to face it sometime, my dear. Let's go hear what the doctor has discovered."

Reluctantly, Harriet took his hand and let him help her from the limo.

"Shall I wait for you, Mr. Douglas?"

"Yes, please, Jonelle. I believe there is a very nice coffee and sandwich shop in the lobby of this building if you are hungry, and parking on the west side. Charge your meal to my account. I'll call you when we need you."

"Thank you, Mr. Douglas. I'll be waiting to hear from you." Jonelle climbed back into the car and drove off.

Harriet watched the limo until its taillights were lost in traffic. She turned to face the modern office building, fighting the sudden nausea that roiled through her belly. Her hands felt cold and clammy. An engraved sign next to the door listed the building's occupants; all were psychiatrists or psychoanalysts.

"I don't want to go in there," she repeated.

Payson took her elbow and guided her toward the entrance. "Look at it this way, Harry. For however long we're in there, it will take your mind off Mark's surgery. Ready?"

Harriet took a deep breath. She was acting like a coward. There were things she needed to know, things about her childhood and her parents. Dr. Ed Bainbridge was the key to recovering those memories.

Nothing had changed since her first visit to the doctor's sumptuous office on the third floor. Her feet sank into the deep green pile carpet. Original oils of Italian scenes graced the pale gold walls. Soft jazz played in the background.

They approached the attractive receptionists—human, not droid—seated behind a crescent-shaped black marble desk. The male looked up. Recognizing Payson, he nodded at them and spoke softly into his headset. They didn't have time to sit before the heavy wooden door at the far end of the reception room opened and Ed Bainbridge came through.

"Payson. Good to see you." The two men shook hands. The doctor nodded at Harriet. She thought he looked a little tired. Fine lines bracketed his eyes and the grooves beside his mouth looked deeper than the last time she'd seen him.

"Harriet. Thank you for coming. Why don't we talk in my office?" He opened and held the door for them, ushering them through with an incline of his head. Harriet smelled his cologne, a pleasant woodsy scent, as she walked past him.

The doctor liked to cook, she remembered suddenly. She didn't know why that felt important, but it made him seem more human. She relaxed slightly, until he turned to speak to the receptionists. "No interruptions," he ordered.

Harriet tried and failed to ignore the chill those two words sent down her spine. Part of her feared what he had to tell her; another part was curious. Was he going to tell her that her memories couldn't be recovered? That the intentionally induced amnesia was permanent?

Or was the doctor about to produce a magic cure? Was today the day that she recalled everything before her eighth birthday?

She avoided looking at the mind-mapping machine that sat in the corner of Bainbridge's office. With its metal cap sprouting hundreds of wires it looked like a horror movie prop. The examination table had been replaced by a brown leather fainting couch that raised and lowered, a small improvement over her previous visit.

The first time Harriet had been in the doctor's office both Payson and Alex had accompanied her. Like then, she automatically chose the middle chair in front of the doctor's desk, one of three cushioned chairs covered in a soft brown and dusky red plaid. Payson sat in the chair to her left, also like before. The empty chair on her right emphasized Alex's absence.

Bainbridge sat behind his modern, green quartz desk and steepled his fingers. "I have good and not-so good news," he said, watching Harriet. "The good news is that I've tracked down the doctor your aunt hired to wipe your memories. His name is McDougall Henry." He waited. When Harriet said nothing he sighed.

"Payson will remember this and you'll find out eventually, so I might as well tell you that McDougall used to be part of this practice. Unfortunately there were some, uh, issues with his patients, and my partners and I were forced to buy him out when he lost his license to practice." He looked at Payson. "You remember Dr. Henry?"

"I do indeed. The scandal would have been before McDougall wiped Harry's memories, though. If he was banished from practice in the States how did Wendolyn Wainwright find him?"

Bainbridge looked uncomfortable. "Henry was banned from practicing here, yes, but that doesn't mean he actually stopped. He did what many unscrupulous professionals do; he took an assumed name, forged credentials, and advertised. I assume Mrs. Wainwright saw his ad and contacted him. Wiping a child's history would have been an opportunity too interesting for Henry to pass up." A look of disgust passed over Bainbridge's face.

"In fact, I tracked down the three professionals still living who might have stolen Harriet's memories–every one of them made the comment that they would have taken the job for the challenge alone. Shmucks."

"Do we trust Harriet's brain to a disgraced practitioner?"

"This is where the not-so good news comes in. McDougall says he can reverse the process." He looked at Harriet, then Payson. "But, no, frankly I don't trust him."

"Why not?" Harriet asked. "Since he's the one that messed with my brain he should be able to reverse the process. Correct?"

Bainbridge tapped his fingers on the desktop. He seemed reluctant to say more. Harriet felt Payson tense beside her.

"Spit it out, Ed. What's the issue?"

"Gully is a drunk. Not only that, he's fallen on hard times. His office is in a poor neighborhood in Mexico City filled with addicts and transients. He claims he can do it, but I think he's only seeing the fee he'll charge. His hands shake. I wouldn't let him touch my worst enemy."

Harriet felt deflated. "That's it then. I'll just have to live with no memories and headaches when I do try to remember."

Bainbridge took a deep breath and let it out on a sigh. "Or you can let me try to help you."

Payson leaned forward in his chair. "If you thought you could help Harry why didn't you offer when we first asked?"

"Because I didn't know then what I know now. Any number of methods could have been used to block Harriet's memories. For me to go blindly rooting around in someone's brain without knowing what I was looking for would have been unethical, not to mention dangerous."

"What's changed?" Harriet asked.

"Before I told Gully about Harriet I took him to dinner and laid a hypothetical case before him. He was happy to talk shop with me. The more he drank, the more he shared about how he would go about wiping a child's memory. Given what he told me, I believe that I can reverse the process." He shrugged. "I definitely know I won't make it any worse. I think it's worth a try."

Payson reached over and grasped Harriet's hand. "It's up to you. What do you think?"

"I don't know what to think. Can you explain the process to me, Dr. Bainbridge?"

"Dr. Henry employed hypnosis and electroconvulsive treatment. I believe that by employing the same methods I can reverse the suggestions he planted in your brain. The good news is that the memories weren't wiped–they're there, just hidden from you."

"Electroconvul–that's shocking the brain with electricity, isn't it?" Harriet shook her head. "I don't like the sound of that."

"The procedure has been greatly refined over the past two hundred years," Bainbridge said. "Most modern practitioners are schooled in its use, although ECT isn't used as often as other treatments."

"What are the side effects and risks?" Payson asked. "Is the treatment worse than the problem?"

Bainbridge nodded. "I'm glad you asked. Memory loss is a biggie, although most–but not all–patients recover most of their memories eventually."

"Then why didn't I?"

"Because Gully also hypnotized you and added an extra layer of insurance, a hypnotic suggestion that whenever a memory threatens to return you will suffer an agonizing headache. Other side effects can be confusion and difficulty focusing, much like attention deficit disorder. Short term you could experience nausea, headaches, confusion–but those generally clear up within a few days."

The thought of someone pulsing an electric current

through her brain made Harriet feel like throwing up. She wasn't sure the cure was worth it. What if she lost even more memories?

"I thought hypnotic suggestions had to be repeated or they eventually fade."

Bainbridge looked pleased by Harriet's observation. "That's normally true; in your case however, Gully used ECT to reinforce the hypnosis. He produced artificial migraines when an image of your parents was shown to you. He asked you for a memory and then zapped you if you recalled it. Eventually the migraine response became automatic; when we think of something repeatedly the brain creates grooves–neural pathways. Gully used that to ensure that every time you tried to remember the past your brain would automatically produce a migraine."

Harriet felt heartsick for her eight year old self. What a horrible thing to do to a child. "This Dr. Henry used hypnosis to reinforce the ECT and then ECT to reinforce the hypnosis? It sounds . . . convoluted and crazy."

"Yeah. I'd apologize for him but it's a little late for that."

"You feel confident that you can reverse the process for Harry?" Payson asked.

"I do, but it's up to Harriet. I won't do it without her consent and willing participation."

"I'd like to sleep on it if that's okay with you, doctor."

"Of course. It's a big decision." Bainbridge pulled a card from his desk and handed it to Harriet. "Call me if you have any questions about the process. I'll try to answer them as best I can." He showed them out of the office.

They waited in silence in the cool shade of the lobby for Jonelle to arrive with the limo. Feeling the need to be alone, Harriet stepped away from Payson and stared unseeing out the window.

The memories her aunt wanted her to forget had to be

horrific if they convinced her aunt to seek out a psychiatrist and let him shoot electricity through her brain–and then follow it up with more pain whenever she tried to remember. If they were that awful did she really want to resurrect them? Wouldn't she be better off not remembering?

A mother with two young children walking past the building caught her eye. The children, a boy and a girl, were holding the mother's hands and skipping. All three looked happy. Was there a time she had ever been that carefree and happy?

Jonelle pulled up and parked in front of the door. Payson appeared at her side. "Are you ready to go back to the hospital?"

Harriet nodded without looking at him and exited the building. She spent the entire ride back to the hospital looking out the window so she wouldn't have to talk to Payson. When the limo pulled up at the hospital entrance Payson remained inside.

"I have some business to attend to. I'll join you later."

Relieved that she would get some time to herself, Harriet waved him off and hurried inside. She stopped at the desk outside the operating theater where they were working on Mark but there was no word yet so she continued on to her room.

Ignoring the cold pizza, she hunted up a glass and poured herself some wine. Gulping it down, she topped off the glass a second time and wrestled a cushioned chair over to the window, which she opened. Sunlight and warm fresh air flooded into the room. She pulled her link from her pocket and saw that she'd missed a call from Solly. She tossed it on the bed. She didn't want to speak with anyone at the moment, not even her closest friend.

How could she knowingly agree to let Dr. Bainbridge

feed electricity into her brain? What if she lost even more memories? Were the earlier ones she had already lost worth the risk?

Eight years of memories–well, more like six, since most people didn't remember anything from their first few years. Six years of memories capped by something so awful that her Aunt Wendy wiped everything. Would a car crash be that bad? She supposed it could if other people died as well. Or if she had been trapped in the car for hours with her dead parents.

She sipped the second glass of wine more slowly as she tried to reason out the situation. She had no relatives that she knew of other than her estranged aunt Wendy. No history. Her name had been changed. What was the name her parents had given her and why had righteous Aunt Wendy felt the need to change it? Her parents had been good people. She knew that in her heart, even though she had no memory of them. The only image she had of her parents, the holo in her office, showed a happy couple, two people who loved each other. And they would have loved her, she felt sure of it.

She pictured the mother she had seen earlier with her two children in front of Bainbridge's office. That's how it would have been with her mother and father. Surely there were many happy memories that had been lost along with the bad ones. She tried to recall an interaction with her parents–any moment at all would do–and was immediately hit with a searing fire that sliced through her skull.

Panting from the pain, she pictured herself running down the beach in front of Mermaid Cottage; the soft, warm breeze, the sound of the gulls, the waves chasing her, the smell of dried seaweed and salt air.

Gradually the pain receded and her breathing slowed.

Yes, there had to be good memories, but the methods

her aunt had employed to obliterate the bad were a neon sign telling Harriet that she needed to be in a strong frame of mind to deal with the past.

Today was not the day. Nor tomorrow. But soon, soon she would be ready.

CHAPTER NINETEEN

Harriet was sound asleep in the chair by the window when a knock on the door woke her. Deep shadows engulfed the hospital courtyard, a sign that hours had passed while she slept. She felt a momentary guilt over the half-empty wine bottle at her feet. Yesterday bourbon, today a bottle of wine. Was she developing a problem? Becoming a lush?

"Eleanor." Harriet held the door open for the resort's doctor. "Come in. How is Mark?" Eleanor looked beat, her eyes red with fatigue. She was still dressed in scrubs. Harriet saw that Payson, or someone doing Payson's bidding, had left a carafe of ice water and a bowl of fruit on the coffee table. She poured a glass and offered it to Eleanor who took it gratefully.

Handing back the empty glass, Eleanor sank onto the edge of the bed. "I could drink another one of those."

Harriet refilled the glass. "Whatever you need. Just ask." She tried to be patient while Eleanor quenched her thirst but it was difficult. Why was the doctor putting off telling her about Mark?

"Mark is stable. We lost him once on the table but we were able to bring him back."

"You . . . lost him." Harriet's knees buckled. She dropped onto the bed beside Eleanor. "Are you saying that Mark died?"

"Technically, yes. He died. There was no heartbeat, so no pulse. But they were able to revive him."

"Thank god," whispered Harriet. "How is his head?"

Eleanor shook her head. "We won't know the extent of the brain damage until the swelling goes down. The surgeons were able to pick all the bone fragments from the brain and cauterize all the bleeders. They attached a synthetic patch to the hole that will stimulate bone growth. If all goes well, Mark's skull will repair itself. That's pretty much all I have to report. Mark has been placed into coma to give his body a chance to focus on the brain."

Mark was in a coma. At least he was alive.

"When can I see him?"

"He's still in recovery. They'll move him to the intensive care unit shortly where they'll monitor him every fifteen minutes through the night, then move him to his room if his vital signs remain stable. I gave the ICU nurses Payson's and your names and said you would probably stop by to see him, but I warn you, he won't know you're there, Harriet."

"I know. But I still need to see him."

"Do you know how he lost his foot?"

"Yes." Harriet hesitated. Would Mark want her to share what she knew? Before she could decide, Payson arrived and saved her from answering. Let Payson tell the doctor about the bomb if she asked again. Harriet slipped out the door while Eleanor was filling him in on Mark's condition and went in search of intensive care.

The intensive care unit occupied a wide, quiet corridor lined with small glass-walled cubicles and a busy nurse's station anchoring the center. Mark's head was swathed in a fat turban of white bandages. His skin still looked gray, the area around his eyes bruised purple.

A monitor near his head constantly flashed his blood pressure, pulse, and heart rhythm. Two clear bags on an IV stand fed into a needle connected to the back of his left hand. Compression sleeves that reminded Harriet of the inflated water wings that children used in the pool covered his legs, clicking on and off as they squeezed and released to keep the blood flowing to prevent clots.

The steady whoosh of the machine that was breathing for him and the click of the compression sleeves were the only sounds in the small room.

Harriet moved a chair next to the bed opposite the medical equipment and found his hand beneath the thin hospital blanket. She held it between both her own. It felt limp, but warm. She knew next to nothing about comas. Was he dreaming? Aware of his surroundings? She cleared her throat.

"Mark? It's me, Harry. Although you told me that you don't like that name and Harriet isn't any better sooooo . . . I don't know what to call myself. I had another name once–you were right about that. Unfortunately I don't remember it. My aunt changed my first name when I went to live with her and my creep uncle. I wonder why she didn't change my last name to match theirs? I never considered that before. If she wanted to obliterate my first eight years why didn't she give me a whole new name instead of just a first name?"

A nurse entered the room on silent shoes. Heavyset, with dark brown hair swept back in a tight bun and a dour expression, she was dressed in scrubs covered with puppies, more suitable for the children's ward than the intensive care unit. The puppies seemed incongruous with her severe manner. She asked for Harriet's name then proceeded to ignore her.

Harriet watched the nurse lift both of Mark's eyelids and flash a bright penlight in them. She checked the compression sleeves and the IV, checked the monitors, and then left as quietly as she had appeared.

"Well, looks like you passed the fifteen minute check. That's good." Harriet's head nodded up and down even though there was no one there to see it. "What are you thinking underneath all those bandages? I feel like I should talk to you and try to draw you out here but the doctors put you in a coma for a reason, so maybe they don't want you to be aware of your surroundings. I think I'll shut up for a while and just sit here if that's okay with you."

Harriet sat quietly through three more nurse check-s.There must have been a shift change because the next nurse was young and talkative, a slim blonde with bright green eyes. Her name tag read Vivian. Vivacious Vivian.

"How is our Mr. Fortner doing?" Vivian asked, as she ran through the same checks the first nurse had done. Harriet wanted to say that Mark didn't belong to the nurse and therefore the term "our" was inappropriate, but she realized that maybe the nurses considered a patient theirs as long as he was under their care.

"I haven't a clue," she answered instead. "He just lies there and ignores me."

Vivian flashed her a grin. "Sometimes that can be a good thing, yes? His vital signs are right where we want them, his pupils are dilating equally so no stroke. Mr. Fortner is doing well under the circumstances. Do you know how he lost his foot?"

"No, I don't." Harriet didn't want to share Mark's personal stories with this stranger, vivacious or not.

"Ah well. Handsome devil, yeah?" Vivian replaced the smaller depleted bag on the IV stand with a new bag, then left.

"Did you hear that, Mark? Vivian called you a handsome devil. She's not wrong. She also said that you're doing well under the circumstances. I wish I knew how Okido managed to sneak up on you. She must have caught you with your thoughts elsewhere. Were you thinking about what a demanding drunk I am? I'm sorry about that, by the way."

Harriet laid her head on Mark's hand. "I'm so confused. I'm attracted to you but . . . there's a big but. I love Alex, I need you to know that." She closed her eyes and waited for the next vitals check.

"Harry." A hand touched her shoulder.

"Mark?" Harriet opened her eyes. Was Mark awake?

"Harry, you need to get some sleep. I'll sit with him."

Not Mark. Payson.

"I spoke to the primary surgeon. He said that they'll keep Mark in a coma overnight and then slowly ease him out of it. Why don't you grab some dinner and head up to your room to sleep? There's a decent bistro in the hospital's lower level or you can order room service. I'll stay with Mark for a while. The nurses know to contact me if there's any change. As soon as I hear anything, I'll contact you."

Harriet didn't want to leave but she sensed that Payson wanted some time alone with Mark. Her stomach growled. She couldn't remember her last decent meal.

"That sounds like a good idea." A hot meal, a shower, and a good night's sleep would go a long way toward making her feel more normal. She would sit with Mark in the morning.

"You'll call me if anything changes?"

"I promise. Go eat and get some rest."

Harriet found a small corner table in the bistro and ordered a hot and sour soup and stir-fry vegetables with rice. As she ate she checked out the other diners. The diners who were there visiting loved ones were easy to pick out. Like her, they were mostly alone and silent, staring into space. Some wiped weepy eyes, looking drained and beaten down.

Most of the diners were obviously hospital staff. They joked and talked and even laughed. Why shouldn't they laugh? They didn't have an emotional connection with their patients. They wouldn't be able to do their job if they did; they needed distance from the suffering they saw every day or they would burn out.

Back in her room, Harriet showered and dressed in a clean tee and underpants to sleep in. Solly had packed her several changes of clothing, bless him. Thinking of her friend reminded her that she owed him a call.

"Thanks for the clean stuff," she said when he answered. "I'd be lost without it."

"Harry! How are you? How's Mark? Tell me everything."

Seeing the concern on Solly's face tipped Harriet over the edge. She wiped tears from her eyes while she told him about the trip over the inland road and Okido's attack. She left out the part about the bourbon and sharing a bed with Mark. When she told Solly about Okido tossing her out of the boat and how she had almost drowned, he shouted at her.

"I should have been there! Why didn't you take me with you?" Harriet let him rail at her until he ran out of steam.

By the time he slowed to a sputter she had her tears under control.

"You were with William. I didn't want to pull you away. Besides, Mark and I didn't think we were chasing down a murderer, we thought we were searching for a missing woman. You know–a helpless victim."

"Harry." She watched Solly choke up, then take a deep breath. "Listen to me. No one, and I do mean no one, can ever be more important to me than you are. You are my best friend and my family. Next time, you call me no matter what I'm doing. Promise?"

Harriet smiled at her friend and blinked back fresh tears. "I promise. What about Okido? Did she get away?"

"Nope. She tried to drown herself but Alex pulled her from the drink. She said there was no point in going on without Alicia."

"Okido told me that Alicia was alive when she last saw her. Can you believe they were going to try to make it look like Dirk Haywood committed suicide?"

Solly shook his head. "Stupid plan. Everyone knows action heroes don't take their own lives unless it's to save someone else's. They're too proud."

"Can you tell Cassie I won't be back in the office for a few days? I want to stay here until I know Mark is out of the woods."

"You've changed your mind about Mark." Solly's brown eyes seemed to peer right through her. "But it's more than that, isn't it? Did something happen last night that you haven't told me?"

Her friend knew her too well. Harriet squirmed while she tried to determine how much she should share. "Maybe. Not really. Let's just say that I'm attracted to him, all right?"

A wide grin split Solly's face. "What do you know. And I suppose you feel guilty because of Alex."

"Of course I do! What kind of woman is attracted to two men at the same time?"

"A normal woman, Harry," Solly said gently. "It happens all the time. There is nothing wrong with feeling attracted to an attractive man. You never had the opportunity to date different men and explore relationships. You had one disastrous relationship and then fell into Alex's arms. Don't beat yourself up over it."

"But I love Alex."

"I know you do. You aren't married to Alex, however. And I'd like to point out that he hasn't asked you to marry him. You've made no commitment to each other. Maybe you should take the opportunity to get to know Mark better. You might discover some things about yourself."

"Like what? That I'm a-a good time girl?" Harriet paced the floor of her room and scowled at her link.

"Harriet."

Harriet stopped walking. When Solly used her full name it meant he was about to get serious.

"I'm listening."

"Good. Look at it this way; if you get to know Mark better you'll give your attraction to Mark the chance to either fizzle out or grow stronger. Otherwise you will always wonder about what might have been."

Harriet mumbled something.

"What?"

"I said I'll think about it."

"That's all I ask. Mark is a good man. So is Alex. Right now Mark needs you and you are right where you should be. The next group of orphans doesn't arrive on the island for another three weeks. Your ads are running and the resort will survive without you being here. I'll clean the perishables from your chiller and send you more clothes if you need them."

"Thanks, Sol. I love you."

"I love you, too. Be gentle with yourself. No one has all the answers, Harry. You'll figure it out as you go along like the rest of us."

CHAPTER TWENTY

When Harriet arrived in the ICU the following morning she discovered that Mark had already been moved to his private room but the nurse refused to divulge any information on his condition.

Harriet tried to calm her nerves while she rode the lift to the top floor. Would Mark be awake? Should she bring up the night they slept together and apologize for getting drunk? Or would it be best to ignore it and pretend it never happened? They hadn't spoken since that night—what if he wanted nothing to do with her?

She breathed a sigh of relief when she found Mark still sleeping. Payson sat at his side sipping a steaming cup of coffee. He nodded toward the flat screen tv, which was on with the sound off.

"The news feeds have the story."

Dirk Haywood's face filled the screen. He looked stoic. Handsome. The camera pulled back and showed him climbing into a sporty black vehicle; the type of car an action hero would drive. An image of a frightened looking

Okido being guided into a police cruiser popped on. Words scrolled across the bottom of the screen.

Famous film producer Alicia Wynn murdered at world's most expensive vacation destination, the Island Resort. Haywood's personal assistant charged with Wynn's death, despite claiming "I'm innocent." A spate of suspicious deaths at the popular resort . . .

Harriet turned away from the screen.

"As you just saw, Alex brought Okido to the mainland this morning for arraignment."

"I hope Dirk wasn't forced to travel with her."

"No. We flew him back last night."

"How is Mark?" Harriet moved to the opposite side of the bed. Alicia was dead, Dirk's life shattered, Okido in custody. There was nothing she could do to change any of it. The Island Resort featured once again in the twenty-four hour news feeds with a story about murder. Frustrating as it was, there was nothing she could do about that either.

"Maybe the resort should institute a policy where all killers caught on the island would be fed to the saltwater crocs. They could put up a sign on the shuttle pad so all arriving guests would be warned."

"Might not be a bad idea, although it could be bad for business."

"Sorry. I'm just frustrated. It was a crazy thought." Time to change the subject. "So, Mark's color looks a little better."

Mark's color did look better, less gray, but he was still unnaturally pale. The heart monitor and breathing tube were still hooked up. The compression sleeves were still on his legs. Only one bag hung from the IV stand.

"They've taken him off the coma-inducing drugs. He hasn't regained consciousness yet but they needed the ICU room so they moved him up here. I've hired a private nurse to check on him every fifteen minutes until Mark wakes."

"Do you have more meetings today?" Payson was dressed in a charcoal gray business suit with a red patterned tie. He looked ready for the office.

"I have to fly up to DC. I won't be back until early evening. You'll stay with Mark so someone will be here when he wakes?"

Harriet agreed. She had nowhere else to be. She thought briefly of Dr. Bainbridge waiting to help her but pushed away the thought. She wasn't ready.

"Have you given any thought to Ed's offer to help you regain your memories?" Payson looked at her over the rim of his coffee mug.

Payson might have been reading her mind. It was all she had thought about. Instead of the good night's sleep she had hoped for, she had spent the night tossing and turning and obsessing either over regaining her memories or her attraction to Mark.

"I did think about it," she admitted. "I-I don't think I'm quite ready." Was that disappointment she saw in Payson's eyes? It was gone so quickly she couldn't be sure. He nodded.

"There's no rush."

They talked about the new ad series she was working on and Chef William's sublime pastries. Payson seemed preoccupied, not listening with one hundred percent of his attention like he usually did. She wondered if the trip to DC was on his mind and what it involved. She felt a tension between them, and then wondered if she was imagining it.

When he stood to go, he kissed Harriet on the cheek. "Call me when Mark wakes. If I can't take the call leave a message. I'll wrap up my business as quickly as I can."

The private nurse came in right after Payson left. An older, capable looking man with a muscular build, shaved head, and a no-nonsense demeanor, he introduced himself as Carl, checked Mark's vital signs and pupils and left.

Harriet picked up Mark's free hand and twined their fingers. She held his hand to her face and lightly rubbed her cheek against the sprinkle of fine dark hairs on his knuckles.

"Did I tell you about Payson's friend, Ed Bainbridge? *Doctor* Ed Bainbridge. He says he can help me recover my memories—maybe. Well, he thinks he can recover them, but there's no guarantee. I don't mind telling you that I'm afraid of what I'll discover about my past so I put it off."

She looked at Mark's still face. The breathing tube looked uncomfortable.

"Something really, really bad happened when I was a child. Something so bad that my aunt had my memories wiped—everything before my eighth year. Who does that unless whatever happened was horrible? Did my mother and father kill someone? Are they alive and in prison?

"Of course the only reason I'm telling you this is because you won't remember a thing I've said. Last night I couldn't even tell Solly that Dr. Bainbridge claims he can help me remember and he's my closest friend. Nor have I told Alex and he's my—well, I'm not sure anymore what he is. I don't think I should discuss Alex with you. It feels disloyal somehow. What else can we talk about?"

Harriet replaced Mark's hand on the bed and stood. Restless, she began to wander around the room. She opened the window a few inches to let in fresh air. The courtyard below was busy. Hospital personnel in scrubs hurried across from one wing to another. Relatives pushed patients in wheelchairs. Two young teens plied their hover boards along the paths. Harriet turned to look at Mark.

"Let's talk about that conversation I overheard between you and Payson. What was that about? What is Payson keeping from Alex? And you said 'them'–that implies he's keeping something from others as well. I heard Payson tell you that he would tell the mysterious 'them' when he was ready. It sounded serious and you did not look happy."

Harriet stopped at the foot of the bed and looked at Mark. "I have the feeling that whatever Payson needs to tell is important, otherwise you wouldn't care. You seemed to know him very well, but that's to be expected given you both work closely with Douglas Wade. A man I have yet to meet, I might add."

She sighed and plopped back into the chair. "It's really none of my business, is it? It was between you and Payson and apparently Alex. And the unnamed 'them', of course."

Carl popped silently in. Harriet watched him check over Mark.

"Have you worked with head injuries before?" she asked.

"Sure. It's amazing how common they are. Why?"

Harriet nodded toward Mark. "Mark had brain surgery and they put him into a coma. Now we're waiting for him to wake up. How long does that take? Can he hear me talking even though he's unconscious? Is he in pain?"

Carl gave her an amused look. His eyes were so blue they were nearly violet.

"One: I don't know. It depends on the patient. Two: some coma patients claim they heard the people around them talking, others don't remember a thing. Three: I have no clue about the pain. You'll have to ask him when he wakes up."

"Fair enough. Thank you."

Harriet sat through another four checks. There was no change in Mark's condition.

"I need some fresh air," she told Carl when he came in next. She gave him her link number and told him to call her immediately if there was any change in Mark's condition.

Outside, the morning was already hot and humid. She moved to the side of the entrance, out of the way of the constant stream of people going in and out of the hospital. It was an insanely busy place. She couldn't even begin to imagine the logistics of keeping track of everything needed to run such a large and complex business.

She began to walk with no clear destination in mind, just a compelling need to be moving. She'd missed her morning run two days in a row and her body felt sluggish, low on oxygen. The crowded sidewalks and stalled traffic didn't help. Horns blared, exhaust fumes choked her. Boomboxes and loud ads from store speakers added to the cacophony. She felt hemmed in, unable to breathe.

She needed to get to a beach and see and smell the water. Hailing a cab, Harriet told the driver to take her to the nearest public beach. Unfamiliar with the city, she had no idea if she had done as asked or driven Harriet to a further destination so she'd receive a larger fare; either way, the ride felt as if it took forever.

Harriet leaped out of the cab, paid the driver, and looked around. The cab had dropped her on the edge of a huge, paved parking lot filled with cars. She spotted a thin strip of water sparkling off to her left and headed that way.

Fifteen minutes later, she stood on the edge of the parking lot and removed her sandals. She had to weave her way between towels and blankets, coolers, beach umbrellas, and people tossing balls and frisbees to get to the water. As far as she could see in either direction, the beach was packed with people, beach toys, and dogs. An intense wave of homesickness for the quiet solitude of Mermaid Cottage washed over her.

She headed back to the parking lot and hailed a cab that was in the process of disgorging a family of five heavily laden with beach paraphernalia and headed back to the hospital.

She found Carl sitting outside Mark's room watching his link. His eyes gleamed when he looked at her.

"Check it out," he said, pointing at the screen. "Even Hollywood's glam aren't safe from the kooks in the world. Dirk Haywood is my fav actor—I never miss his films."

Harriet caught a glimpse of the news footage of the famous action hero that she'd been seeing all morning. She mumbled something to Carl and fled into Mark's room, closing the door behind her. Leaning her forehead against the door, she took several deep breaths to collect herself.

Knowing the buzzards who manned the news feeds were talking about murder on the resort while she was distanced by the seclusion of the island felt far different from having it shoved in her face everywhere she went on the mainland.

The cab driver on the journey from the beach to the hospital had it streaming on her in-dash screen and could talk about nothing else. Buses and air trams streamed it on their sides—maximum exposure real estate sold to the relentless media companies who wanted to get as many eyes on their pieces as possible. Retail windows streamed the story; digital billboards flashed on the roofs of buildings and from empty lots.

There was no escape from the tragedy of Alicia Wynn's death. Poor Dirk. She couldn't imagine how painful it had to be for him, to see his dead wife's face everywhere he went.

Harriet straightened away from the door and turned.

Mark's breathing tube and the IV bag of drugs had been removed although they were still pumping fluids into him. The compression sleeves remained on his legs and probably would until he was up and walking on his own.

Someone had turned on the flat screen tv and closed the window. The room felt close and stuffy and smelled of disinfectant. She snapped off the tv, which–of course featured talking heads discussing Alicia Wynn and the popular actor Dirk Haywood. *Such a Tragedy!* She opened the window again, then sat in the chair beside Mark's bed and took his hand.

"I'm back," she said, forcing as much upbeat cheer into her voice as she could muster. "It's hell out there. Be glad you're sequestered in this nice, quiet oasis."

A two day beard showed dark against Mark's skin and the white bandages wrapped around his skull. She reached out a finger and gently traced the hook of his nose, ran the back of her hand down his cheek. Tiny blue capillaries crisscrossed his eyelids. His eyes were moving beneath them. Was he dreaming? Waking up?

"Mark? Can you hear me? Open your eyes and look at me." Harriet waited several minutes but Mark gave no sign he could hear her. A sudden wave of exhaustion washed through her body. The last two days had been an emotional rollercoaster. She felt tapped out.

"I think I need to take a nap. I'm so tired I can barely sit up. I'll come back soon, I promise. Carl is sitting right outside the door and he'll check on you every quarter hour. If you need anything have him call me and I'll come right away. I'll be back in a couple hours." Harriet kissed Mark's cheek and left the room.

CHAPTER TWENTY-ONE

Harriet was having trouble setting one foot in front of the other by the time she made it to her room. It took her three tries to enter the door code. Dropping her backpack to the floor just inside the door, she stumbled to the bed and fell onto it face down. She must have fallen asleep immediately because when she opened her eyes she was still fully dressed, including her shoes.

"Ugh." Harriet rolled to her back and waited for her brain to kick into gear. A glance at the window told her it was early evening. She had slept for several hours. She needed to get back to Mark's room, but not without a shower first. She felt sticky and stale and her clothes smelled of sweat and bus fumes and taxi.

She set the room coffee pot to perking and jumped into the shower. Thirty minutes later she was showered, dressed in clean jeans and a pale green silk tee, and buzzing with caffeine. She grabbed her backpack off the floor and headed across the hospital.

The hospital had been constructed in several phases over many decades. The wing of private rooms for visitors was the most recent addition. Harriet passed from its brightly lit, spacious halls to the dimmer, more narrow passages in the hospital's oldest section. The floors were clean but obviously worn, the linoleum scratched and dull. Housekeeping carts created an obstacle course even though the cleaners parked them up tight against the walls.

Every once in a while a room door would be open, giving Harriet a glimpse of a body under a white sheet in the dim light and a soundless tv screen flashing images to a patient who was most likely unaware. This was the wing and floor for the terminal patients, mostly the elderly who still had some funds and family who chose not to keep them at home. They were here for one reason only, with no hope of extending their lives.

Harriet hurried down the hall as quietly as possible. A metal framed double door led into the newer wing that housed surgery and the ICU on the fourth and fifth floors. Semi-private rooms occupied floors six through fourteen. Like the rooms Payson had secured for himself and Harriet, Mark's private room was on the top floor.

Two female and a male nurse were seated at the nurse's station when Harriet approached. She introduced herself and asked if there was any change in Mark's status before heading to his room. The nurse she spoke with first refused to share any information until she checked Mark's chart and saw that Harriet was listed as family.

Payson's doing, Harriet was sure. She was grateful that he'd thought to include her name on the forms.

According to the nurse, Mark had not opened his eyes nor spoken yet but his vitals were all within acceptable range for his condition. No, she had no idea how long it would take for him to regain consciousness, every patient was different. She suggested that Harriet go sit with Mark and wait.

With a great deal of effort, Harriet stifled her frustration at the lack of information and headed to Mark's room. The lights had been partially dimmed for the night but Harriet saw that Carl's chair was empty which meant he was checking on Mark. She slowed her steps to give him time to finish but he still hadn't emerged by the time she reached Mark's door. Pasting a smile on her face, Harriet stepped into the room.

Except for the rectangle of light from the hallway, the room was dark.

"Carl?" A body stood next to the bed, leaning over Mark.

"Carl? Is everything all right? Why did you turn off the lights?"

The body straightened and turned toward Harriet. The glow of the call button cast a faint glow on his face and the pillow in his hands. She stepped closer to the bed, saw that Mark's visitor wasn't Carl.

"Dirk? What a surprise. What are you doing here?"

"I was just checking on your friend," Dirk Haywood said smoothly. "I heard what Okido did to him and I wanted to see if there was anything I could do for him."

"That was-that was very kind of you. Do you know where Carl is? He should be outside the door." Something felt wrong, but Harriet was having a difficult time putting her finger on just what that was. Haywood took a step closer to her. He still had the pillow clutched between his hands.

Pillow. He'd been leaning over Mark with a pillow.

The breath whooshed out of Harriet's body as understanding flooded in. "Okido was hiding in the boat, waiting for the seas to calm enough to get away. I thought she was trying to escape after killing Alicia, but she insisted Alicia was alive when she dropped her on the beach. She was hiding from you, wasn't she?"

Haywood's face was expressionless. She glanced at the door, hoping Carl had returned, but the hallway was empty. Haywood took another step closer to her.

"You took the Hog, not Okido. You killed Alicia," Harriet whispered. "You killed your wife and you hit Mark with a rock. Why? Why would you do that?"

"Do you have any idea what it would do to my reputation if the news media discovered that my wife and Okido had been lovers *while we were married*? I'd become a laughingstock. The butt of late night show jokes. I can see the headlines now. 'Action hero can't keep wife satisfied.' It would have killed my career."

"How did you find out?" Where was Carl? If only he'd come back. She glanced at Mark. His eyes were closed but she saw his chest rising and falling. She'd arrived before Haywood could smother him.

An ugly laugh that sent a chill down Harriet's spine escaped Haywood's lips. "That bitch wife of mine told me. She confessed the whole plan to me in an effort to come clean so we could start over. Said she had broken it off with Okido. As if that made any difference. Stupid –." He spit out a string of unpleasant words. "Did you know they planned to kill me and make it look like a suicide?"

Harriet recalled someone describing Haywood as stoic and proud. They'd had the right of it. Pride had made Haywood kill his wife. "You killed your wife *after she told you that she wanted to try to make your marriage work.*"

Haywood either didn't hear or ignored her. "They were going to make it look like I took my own life." He thumped his chest with one fist. "I'm the top action hero in films, for chrissakes. I would never take my own life. They had to pay."

"How did you get to the east side of the island and back?"

"Ran. Hiked. I keep in good shape. Have to for my films. I usually run six or more miles a day. Crossing the island was nothing. Alicia told me Okido was hiding there."

"And now you're here to kill Mark."

"Unfortunate, but he saw me on the rocks when I was searching for Okido. I told him I had come to help, waited for him to turn his back, and hit him. I'm afraid he'll remember when he wakes so I can't let that happen, obviously."

"And Okido?" Where the hell had Carl gone off to? Haywood was inching closer. "You'd let her go to prison for a murder she didn't commit?"

"Absolutely. Once she's locked away I'll arrange for a little 'accident' for her."

Harriet made a dash for the door. Haywood sprang at her and caught her by the calves, bringing her down before she could reach it. She smashed her right elbow into the floor when she fell. Intense pain shot up and down her arm. Tears blurred her vision.

Haywood jumped up and shut and locked the door. "It's too bad you had to arrive when you did. Another minute I would have been out of here and everyone would assume Mark died from his head injury. They will still assume that, since I'll finish what I started once I deal with you."

Gripping her elbow, Harriet sat up. "You can't kill me and make it look like an accident. Carl will find you here."

"Carl is gone. Never forget that everyone has their price. I found Carl's and told him to get lost for the remainder of the night. He was eager to oblige his favorite action hero."

There would be no help from that quarter then. Harriet

blinked away the tears and stood slowly, still rubbing her elbow. "I won't let you kill Mark," she said quietly.

"You have nothing to say about it." Haywood grabbed her left bicep and squeezed hard. "I'm sure the news media will come up with a good story." He half pushed, half dragged her toward the window.

"How does this sound? 'Love sick resort employee throws herself out window.' Even better, 'Woman finds lover dead, throws herself out window.' You see the general theme here, don't you?"

Harriet let her legs sag until she was dead weight and dug her heels in, but Haywood was too strong for her. His fingers dug deeper into her bicep. He reached the window and shoved it open as far as it would go, then grabbed her under the arms and lifted her into the opening.

Harriet screamed and scratched at Dirk's eyes and face. At least she'd have some of Haywood's DNA under her nails when she was found. He wouldn't get away with her murder; Alex would know she'd never jump from a window.

"Bitch!" Dirk grabbed her left shin. With one hand gripping her left bicep and one on her shin he lifted her whole body until she was level with the window sill.

Harriet heard someone behind them. She tried to turn to look but Haywood 's shoulders blocked her. She looked down and saw the lighted paths in the courtyard fourteen stories below and wondered at the irony. She finally had a chance to remember her past only to be murdered before she retrieved a single memory.

Haywood dropped her suddenly. The sill caught Harriet in the stomach. She reached back until she found the edges of the window and shoved her body back inside the room.

When she turned to see what had stopped Haywood

she saw Mark lying on the floor in the middle of the room with his blanket half-wrapped around his legs and trailing back to the bed. His IV stand lay on the floor beside him. Haywood was swearing and bleeding from the scalp.

Someone pounded on the door. "Open this door," came the muffled voice of the nurse Harriet had spoken to earlier.

"Help! Call the police!" Harriet shouted.

Haywood dropped to his knees beside Mark and grabbed Mark's throat with both hands. Harriet picked up the closest weapon she could find–the metal bedpan from the shelf next to the bed–and swung it as hard as she could at the actor's head. He collapsed on top of Mark.

The bedpan dropped from her hand with a loud clatter. She rolled Haywood's still body off Mark, then ran and unlocked the door. All three nurses piled into the room. They moved Harriet out of the way and gently lifted Mark back onto the bed.

"What happened here? Hey, isn't that Dirk Haywood?"

"Did you call the police?" Harriet asked.

"I called hospital security," the male nurse answered.

"Not good enough." Harriet retrieved her backpack and pulled out her link. She dialed the emergency number for the police and went to stand out of the way in the corner of the room to wait while the nurses fussed over Mark.

Hospital security showed up first. Harriet explained that she had found Haywood trying to smother Mark with a pillow and she had already called the police. The full story could wait until they showed up.

The nurses checked Mark over carefully. One righted the IV stand and reattached it to the port in his hand. Another checked his bandages for seepage and the third called the surgeon.

Mark neither moved nor opened his eyes during all this.

"How did the patient end up on the floor?" asked the male nurse.

"I don't know. I couldn't see." The chair beside the bed had gotten knocked over. Harriet righted it. Afraid her legs would no longer support her, she sat and waited for the police to arrive.

CHAPTER TWENTY-TWO

"Throat." The whisper was so soft she almost missed it. The police had come and gone, taking Dirk Haywood with them. Mark had slept through it all.

"Your throat hurts? That would be from the breathing tube, I suspect. Let me give you some water. Just relax while I guide the straw between your lips." She poured water from a waiting plastic carafe into the sip cup and guided the straw into Mark's mouth. He sucked greedily until she pulled the cup away.

"Not too much. I'd better tell the doctor you're awake. Be right back." She rang the call button on the bed and asked the responding nurse to fetch Mark's doctor, then she left a message for Payson on his link.

"I'm sure everyone will be happy to have you back with us," she said, taking the seat beside the bed and picking up Mark's hand again. "You gave me quite a scare you know. Haywood tried to kill you. We thought it was Okido at first. If I hadn't shown up when I did–" she shuddered. "It doesn't matter now."

The nurse arrived with the doctor. While the surgeon

flashed a light in Mark's eyes he introduced himself as Dr. Cutter–no jokes please–and explained that Dr. Clarke had returned to the island and he was now in charge of Mark's well-being.

He turned off his light, squeezed Mark's fingers and toes, then poked his palms and the soles of Mark's foot with the end of a pen. "Can you feel this? How about when I do this?" He wrote something on Mark's chart, pronounced him on the mend, and said he'd check back in a few hours.

When they were alone again Harriet sat and smiled. Mark's dark eyes were open and watching her.

"Hi there," she said softly. "I was afraid you weren't going to make it. You looked pretty bad when I found you. I guess we're even now since you just saved my life."

"Where did you find me? What happened?"

Harriet hesitated. During the shuttle ride to the hospital Eleanor had warned her that Mark might have blank spots when he regained consciousness. She had also warned Harriet that it was important not to upset him until he'd regained his strength.

But Dr. Clarke didn't know Mark as well as Harriet did; she didn't know what a strong will he had.

"Do you remember being on the island? We were searching for a missing woman. I thought she hit you on the head from behind with a rock but I was wrong. Dirk Haywood hit you. He also killed his wife and was searching for Okido to kill her and then he tried to kill you."

Mark frowned. "I saw him when I went to check the other cabins."

"So he told me. He was afraid you would realize he was hunting down Okido so he knocked you out and took your blade so you couldn't run away while he took care of his personal assistant. Fortunately I showed up and found you and called Tarbell."

"Head hurts."

"Not surprising. The rock crushed a portion of your skull. You had surgery yesterday to remove bone fragments."

"What hospital is this?"

"Miami All-Saints. You're in a private room on the top floor. Payson arranged it for you."

"Payson?" A small furrow appeared between Mark's eyes and then cleared. "Oh. You mean Douglas."

"Yes. He would be here but he had to go to DC today. I'm sure he'll check on you as soon as he returns."

Harriet tried not to blush or fidget while Mark inspected her face. She wasn't used to such close scrutiny; it made her want to squirm in her seat. She rubbed the bump on her nose. Once, in a fit of insecurity, she had asked Solly if she was pretty. He had replied that it was the beauty within that counted, not the stuff on the surface. She had taken his answer as confirmation that she was not a pretty woman.

She forced herself to drop her hand to her lap.

"I know you from the resort, don't I?" Mark's voice broke and turned into a dry, hacking cough. He tried to reach for the sip cup but missed. Harriet stood and held it to his lips. He relaxed his head back against the pillow and looked at her through half-lowered eyelids.

"You don't remember me?" she asked.

"Of course I do. I just can't think of your name. You're behaving as if we're close, but I know that's not true. You do have a name, I assume?" Mark added drily.

Here was the arrogant tone she associated with Mark Fortner, chief financial officer for the wealthiest man on the planet. She clenched her fingers and glared at him.

"Of course I have a name. It's Harriet Monroe." She heard a woman's voice–her mother's?–calling her by a different name. "Twinkle," she whispered. She breathed through the dull throb that threatened to turn into real pain. Please, let her at least remember her name.

"My name is Twinkle." Her tongue tripped over the name but it felt right. Mark barked out a laugh and then groaned. "Ow, that hurt. You're putting me on. Who would name their baby girl Twinkle?"

"My parents, obviously." Her name was Twinkle Monroe–she felt sure of it. She didn't know how her name had slipped through the blocks in her brain but she clung to it; a lifeline to her past. Twinkle Monroe. Now that she knew it, she would never forget.

The pain in her skull grew stronger. It was time to think of something else. Fortunately Mark was there to help her out.

"Twinkle, twinkle, little star. I like it. It suits those unusual blue eyes of yours. You obviously know who I am, so maybe now you'll explain why you're sitting beside my bed."

"I told you. We were–"

"Yeah, I heard you. We were searching for a woman, blah, blah. Why were you and I searching together and where did you say this was?"

"On the island. Just how much *do* you remember, Mark?" Mark closed his eyes and ignored the question. She thought he had fallen asleep when he spoke again.

"What island?"

"The Island Resort. I work there." Harriet frowned. Was it normal for a head injury patient's memories to fade in and out?

"Ah, yes. Now I remember. I went to the resort to check

over the financials for Doug. I met Dirk Haywood there. Helluva guy. Stoic. Proud."

Doug. Mark knew Douglas Wade well enough to call him Doug. She was sure he had to be one of a very few who were that familiar with the reclusive multi-billionaire.

"Haywood's wife was murdered and his personal assistant disappeared. You and I were searching for her," Harriet prompted.

"We drove one of the Hogs over the road through the jungle."

"That's right! You do remember." Did he also remember the things he had said to her during the trip across the island? Did he remember the bourbon and sharing a bed? She didn't dare ask.

Mark remained quiet for several minutes. Harriet could practically see the gears turning in his brain. Suddenly he opened his eyes, whipped the blanket off his legs, and groaned.

"Damn. I was hoping the bomb was part of a bad dream. It appears that I am still not a whole man." He pulled the blanket back over himself and closed his eyes again. "Thank you for saving my life, Twink. I'll see that you're suitably rewarded. There's no need to wait around for it; I promise I won't forget."

For a moment Harriet was too shocked to speak, but only for a moment. Anger flooded her body. She heard the door open behind her but didn't care if the nurse overheard her.

"You insufferable boor. I don't want anything for saving your miserable, arrogant hide."

"Am I interrupting something?"

Harriet whipped around. Payson stood in the open door with an amused expression on his face.

"Awake for–" he checked his wrist unit–"less than an

hour and I see you're back to being your usual charming self, Mark."

"Doug. Glad to see you. Escort this female from my room, will you? She's tiring me out with all her chatter."

He didn't really want her to leave. Seeing Harriet sitting beside his bed had filled Mark with pleasure and a longing that had threatened to overwhelm him. He would have liked nothing better than to pull her down onto the bed with him and snuggle the way he'd snuggled with her in the cottage. He had pretended to have a spotty memory in the hopes she wouldn't bring up that night.

He'd meant it when he said he wasn't a whole man. He also wasn't a particularly good man where women were concerned. Twinkle Harriet Monroe was a good woman, the best he'd ever known; a woman who deserved much more than he could ever give her. He knew himself, knew that faithful was not part of his vocabulary. Eventually she would end up hating him and he couldn't bear that.

"I don't need a bloody escort. I'm happy to leave." Harriet blinked back the tears pressing against her eyes. Mark's unexpected cold dismissal had shocked and hurt. She stood to leave and squared her shoulders. Her arm hurt where Haywood had grabbed her. Her other arm hurt where Okido had sliced her. Her elbow still throbbed. And now Mark had wounded her with a quick, deep jab to her heart.

The guy was a jerk and definitely not worth crying over. She'd been so wrong about him. She needed to be alone, needed to lock herself in her room and absorb everything that had happened. And then she needed to get home to the island.

Halfway to the door, she stopped. She stared at Payson, who was still standing in the doorway with a strange expression on his face.

"He called you Doug." It was all so blindingly obvious now. The second bedroom in Payson's cottage filled with sophisticated electronics. How Douglas Wade had known about her destroyed wooden hippo collection and replaced it. How he seemed to know everything happening on the island as soon as it happened.

"Payson? He called you Doug." Resignation replaced the strange expression on Payson's face.

"It's Payson Douglas Wade, actually. I was going to tell you. I just hadn't found the right moment." He came into the room and closed the door behind him. When he turned back to Harriet he had regained his composure. His gaze was steady, his tone matter of fact.

"As soon as a person realizes they're dealing with the richest man on the planet, everything changes. I didn't want my money to affect our friendship." He held out a hand. "I'm truly sorry for the deception. Can you forgive me?"

Harriet took a step back. "Mark tried to tell you to come clean about your real identity that day we were searching the cove for Okido. I'm one of the 'them' he was referring to. Solly and Alex must be the others."

Payson's eyes were steady on hers. "I'm the same person you knew as Payson Douglas. There's just a little more to me than you realized. The deception is necessary, Harry. On the island I can live my life without people pestering me for money or trying to sell me on business partnerships. Do you think I'd get even one day of peace if anyone knew I was there? Not to mention how the news media would be constantly trying to sneak onto the resort trying to get a photo of me?"

Harriet took a deep breath and let it out. "No," she admitted. "I suppose it's difficult for you to live any kind of normal life."

"And would you have agreed to have lunch with me on Thursdays if you didn't think of me as a lonely old man?"

Harriet looked at the man she had grown to think of as the kindly uncle she'd never had. She was inordinately fond–protective even–of Payson. Did that change with this new knowledge?

"You could have trusted me."

"Harry, I've spent a lifetime amassing and protecting my empire. For what should be obvious reasons trust does not come easy. It's earned. Mark was right that day you overheard us. I would have told you sooner rather than later. This is not how I wanted you to find out. But now that you have, I have to ask you to keep my secret. Payson Douglas can travel the world unremarked. I need that secret identity."

"I'm insulted that you think I'd go blabbing."

"I didn't really think you would." He approached Harriet and pulled her in for a gentle hug. "I promise I'll tell Alex and Solly as soon as we get back to the island."

Harriet heard Mark grumbling behind her back. "Twinkle's too young for you, Doug." She felt Payson stiffen against her. He gripped her upper arms and pushed her away, searching her face. She gasped from the pain when he squeezed her cut arm. Payson released her immediately but continued to stare at her.

"Mark just called you Twinkle."

Harriet's grin was rueful. "I guess it's a day for revealing secret names."

"How?"

"I don't know." She shrugged one shoulder. "Maybe our visit to Dr. Bainbridge's office created a small rift in the blocks Dr. Henry placed in my brain. Maybe Henry's methods are starting to break down. I don't know."

Payson walked to the window and stood with his back

to the room. Despite having his hands in his pockets and his deliberate, relaxed stance, she detected the tension in his slim body.

"Is that all you've remembered?"

"Yes. I tried for more but the pain is immediate. I can't explain how my name slipped through."

Harriet glanced at Mark and saw that he was watching them with a puzzled look on his face. "What am I missing here?" he asked.

"Nothing," replied Harriet.

"It doesn't feel like nothing." He was staring hard at Harriet. "Everyone on the island calls you Harriet or Harry. You just admitted that you didn't know your name is Twinkle until today. How can that be?"

"I told you my brain is broken." Before she could say more, Dr. Cutter arrived.

"I understand you wanted to see me, Mr. Douglas?"

"Yes. How soon before Mr. Fortner can travel? I have a private shuttle on standby and will hire whatever medical or nursing care he needs. Given the news media will soon learn about Haywood and be hounding the hospital for access to Mr. Fortner before morning, I believe he'll recuperate faster at home."

The doctor grimaced at the mention of the news media. "I'll release him to home health care in the morning, as long as his vitals remain stable overnight."

"Thank you, doctor. I'll make the appropriate arrangements."

"So," Mark said, as soon as the door closed behind the doctor. "Your brain is broken how?"

Harriet still smarted from Mark's callous words and didn't feel like talking anymore. "You wanted me to leave. I'm gone."

She left before Mark or Payson could say anything and

hurried back to her room where she tossed her clothes into the duffle Solly had sent. Her link buzzed before she finished. Checking caller i.d. she saw that it was Alex.

"Alex." Tears flooded Harriet's eyes. "Where are you?"

"On my way to you. I brought Okido to the mainland to turn her over to the authorities and I'm en route to the hospital."

"Okido didn't kill Alicia. Or hurt Mark. It was Haywood. He was arrested less than an hour ago."

"What? How do you know? What happened? Never mind, I'll be there shortly. Where can I find you?"

Harriet ceased packing and sat to wait for Alex. While she waited she thought about Mark and what to tell Alex. By the time he knocked on her door she'd decided there was nothing to tell. She had experienced a short infatuation for the chief financial officer. Nothing inappropriate had happened. End of story.

She opened the door to Alex and stepped into his arms, holding him tight. "I have so much to tell you. Starting with," she took a deep breath, "I've remembered my name."

Without releasing her, Alex pushed Harriet inside and closed the door to her room with his foot. He picked her up and headed for the chair. She'd forgotten how strong he was. He sat and pulled her into his lap. After kissing her thoroughly he tipped her chin up.

"I've missed you," he said. He kissed the tip of her nose, her temples, her forehead, her lips again, then sat back, pulling her against his chest. Harriet released a long sigh, safe and secure in his arms.

"Tell me all. Start at the beginning."

She gathered her thoughts, and started at the beginning.

* * *

For the the first word about releases, sales, news, and special notices, sign up for my newsletter. https://charleymarshbooks.com/mystery-newsletter/

Get your copy now of the next book in the Destination Death Mystery Series Coming April 2022 *Betrayed in Paradise*

https://books2read.com/BetrayedinParadise

Turn the page for a preview of the next book in the Destination Death series, *Betrayed in Paradise.*

BETRAYED IN PARADISE

Two blissful months. Sixty-five days without a murder, mayhem, or even a serious injury at the Island Resort. Harriet Monroe wished it would last indefinitely, but she felt fairly certain that she herself was going to commit murder in the next day or two.

She often took on special projects to help Cassandra Montgomery–the resort manager–because she enjoyed a challenge. It took anticipation, hard work, and focused dedication to meet all the guests' needs–and never more so than when a wedding was involved.

This particular wedding, however, was fast becoming the straw that broke her back, or rather, the event that finally put her in the camp of "if this one person no longer walked the earth, my life would be so much better."

The bride to be's mother called several times a day and had been doing so for the previous two months, after her daughter and soon to be son-in-law had decided the large family vacation/reunion at the resort would be the perfect time and place to get married.

Harriet had felt excited about the wedding when Cassie

first asked her to pull it together. Weddings were a time of joy, an excuse to get the family and close friends together and party. Fun times. How much more difficult could it be to expand a family reunion into a wedding?

Oodles more difficult, as it turned out.

Not because of the bride and groom, who were a *lovely* couple, a couple who insisted they wanted a simple marriage ceremony and a multi-tiered chocolate cake with mocha frosting and minimal decoration. Unfortunately Marolyn Packard, a.k.a. Mother of the Bride, decided the wedding had to incorporate every new idea that came to her attention. And because Marolyn obsessively stalked every wedding website to grace the internet–tasteful or atrocious–many bizarre and impractical ideas came to her attention.

Worse, Marolyn changed her mind several times a day and kept Harriet informed of every consideration, no matter how silly.

"I want Victoria to ride a white stallion to the altar on the beach," Marolyn gushed. *"It will be so romantic."* Never mind that Victoria was frightened of horses and, other than chickens, the World Wildlife Sanctuary prohibited bringing domestic livestock to the island.

"I want a chocolate fountain. It was all the rage fifty years ago. I'll be reigniting a trend." There was a reason the trend had died. Harriet pictured the chocolate-covered insects that would fill the fountain within minutes.

"Yellow roses."

"Stargazer lilies. No, I changed my mind. Lilies are for funerals."

"Purple pansies."

Every day a different flower for the table arrangements and bridal bouquet. It had become a running joke between

Harriet and Solly, who was in charge of the resort's seven greenhouses.

"I want to release a thousand blue and white butterflies when they're pronounced man and wife." (Again, prohibited by the World Wildlife Sanctuary.)

"She changed her mind about the flowers again," Harriet told Solly when he answered his link. There was no need to identify "she" by name. Solly shook his head and sighed.

"What's the new flower of the day? Marolyn does realize the wedding takes place day after tomorrow?"

"She does. Lily of the Valley."

"Ooh. That's a brilliant choice for the bride's bouquet, actually. I'll do it. Tell Marolyn it's too late to change her mind again if she tries. I'm going to mix in island flowers for the table bud vases and the arch and we're done. Have you talked to the bride about her mother's flower choice?"

"As it happens, Lily of the Valley was Victoria's first choice. Marolyn overruled her, but eventually came around. Will you need extra hands to set everything up? I can find some volunteers if you do."

"Nope. We've got it." Solly plus his greenhouse crew of eight made nine sets of hands. Harriet checked Flowers off her list.

"Any chance you and William can come to dinner tonight?"

Solly raised one eyebrow. "You cooking? Last time you invited us didn't work out so well. If I remember right, you turned sweet, succulent shrimp into little bits of dry, pink rubber."

Harriet stuck her tongue out at Solly's smirking face. So far, her recent attempts to master more than eggs and sandwiches had been an unmitigated disaster. "Yes, I'm cooking."

"Order extra garlic bread for me and William." He smirked and hung up before Harriet could think of a comeback. That was the trouble with having a close friend who knew you almost as well as they knew themselves. Solly guessed correctly that she wouldn't attempt to cook again so soon after her last disastrous attempt. She sighed and called the employee canteen to order takeout for four.

Harriet's link buzzed as soon as she ended the call to the canteen. She decided not to answer if it was Marolyn again, but when she checked the screen she saw the caller was Victoria's maid of honor, Cynn Gaudreau.

"Miss Gaudreau. What can I do for you?"

Cynn's face popped on the screen. Her short, spiky, bright red hair, up-tilted green eyes, and pointed chin made Harriet think of elves. The illusion shattered as soon as Cynn spoke. Her voice had a breathy, sex symbol quality to it that made her sound as if she was in the throes of an orgasm—or about to die from lack of oxygen.

Harriet sympathized with the bride's best friend. Cynn was in an untenable position, caught between Victoria and Victoria's mother.

"It's Marolyn, Harry. Can you talk to her? The maid of honor is supposed to host the bridal shower, but Vic's mother keeps calling me and telling me what to do. I told her I have it under control but she doesn't listen. I have a plan. She needs to leave me alone."

"I thought the bridal shower was tonight."

"It is! Even if I agreed with Marolyn, it's too late to change my plans again. I wanted to take Vic and her closest cousins out on the excursion party boat, but Marolyn insists that I have the shower on the rooftop restaurant. Can't you make Vic's mother see reason?"

Harriet could empathize, but she didn't want to be sucked into the role of peacekeeper. She had enough on her plate and her own problems with Marolyn. She carried her link over to the French doors that opened onto a lanai and the beach and stared out at the sparkling turquoise water. A large group of youngsters dashed in and out of the waves, screaming and shouting at the top of their voices.

"I understand how frustrated you must be, Miss Gaudreau, but it's not my place to speak to Mrs. Packard. Perhaps you should ask Victoria to have a word with her mother. Or speak to Mr. Packard."

"No! Vic thinks I can handle her mother. That's why she chose me to be her maid of honor. Forget it. I'll think of something." She hung up before Harriet could say anything more.

The family and wedding party had arrived two days before, filling every available room and cottage on the west side of the island. Because she had been fielding calls from them for nearly two months, Harriet had greeted them at the shuttle pad, feeling that it was important to meet the bride and groom, the bride's parents, and the maid of honor in person.

Big mistake. Her link had rung almost non-stop since that meet and greet. For some reason, Marolyn and Cynn thought of her as their personal attendant, a general dogsbody.

"I'll need someone to do Victoria's and my hair."

Harriet suggested Marolyn contact the spa and see if someone there could oblige.

"I have several outfits that will need to be cleaned."

Call the hotel concierge, Cynn.

The beach rang with the shouts of the youngsters playing in the water. All were all first and second cousins, many meeting for the first time. Harriet wondered what that would feel like–to have an extended family so large they filled all the resort's available rooms. She did a quick calculation—that was well over three hundred guests. Other than the maid of honor, the groom and his immediate family and the best man, all the resort guests were related.

Harriet had exactly two living relatives she was aware of and she had cut all ties with them when she was fifteen. Solly was her family, another runaway she had bonded with and kept. Happily, a few of her resort co-workers had become family as well.

A figure in a large straw sunhat stalking toward the office building from the beach caught Harriet's eye. Marolyn Packard.

"Oh, no you don't." Harriet shut down her computer and turned off the office lights, then stood next to the window where Marolyn couldn't see her. If she didn't think Marolyn would notice the movement, she'd have closed her drapes.

A broad shadow in a floppy hat crept across the floor until it covered her desk. Harriet held her breath, sure that somehow Marolyn could feel her presence. Too late, she realized she had left the small canvas pack she preferred carrying over a pocketbook on the floor next to the desk—and her sandals lay in a jumble beneath the elegant rosewood desk.

Harriet stifled a groan when Marolyn knocked on the glass and called her name.

"Harry! Harry, I need to talk to you about the bridal shower." The annoying knocking continued. "Harry! I know you're in there. I need to talk to you now."

Not a chance. This was something Marolyn and Cynn needed to work out themselves. Referee was not in her job description. Harriet closed her eyes and waited for

Marolyn to go away. She heard the neighboring office's French door open and Cassie's voice on the lanai.

Damn. The woman had been speaking loud enough to disturb the resort manager. She was going to have to go out there and deal with Marolyn.

Cassie's broader shadow joined Marolyn's.

"Excuse me, Mrs. Packard." Cassie's tone through the glass was polite but firm. "These offices are off limits to guests."

Harriet held her breath and waited.

"But I need to speak with Harry and she isn't answering her link."

"Then she must be tied up with something or someone. I suggest you leave Harriet a message. She's a very busy person, but I'm sure she'll get back to you as soon as she can."

Marolyn tried to argue. Harriet watched Cassie's shadow take the other woman's arm and lead her off the lanai. The office manager's French door closed several minutes later. Harriet's link buzzed in her hand. She let it go to voice mail when she saw Marolyn's name. It buzzed again. Cassie's name popped up on the screen.

"Cassie! Thank you for dealing with Mrs. Packard. The woman calls me practically every twenty minutes."

"You can stop hiding. And don't thank me—it's the least I can do after foisting the annoying woman on you. I swear, I had no idea how awful she was going to be."

Harriet peered around the edge of the glass and scanned the beach. Marolyn stood near the water with her hands on her hips. From the body language, Harriet guessed she was scolding the kids for something. Several stood knee-deep in the water, staring at their feet. A half-dozen were sneaking away behind Marolyn. It looked like

Harriet wasn't the only one trying to avoid the bride's mother.

"You had no idea Marolyn was a control freak of epic proportions? Somehow I find that hard to believe. You must have spoken with her when she booked the resort for the family reunion."

"Fine. I knew." Cassie huffed out a sigh. "I owe you one."

"And you can be sure I will collect."

The women grinned at one another and Harriet ended the call. She listened to Marolyn's message and erased it. It was too late to make any significant changes to the bridal shower. She only hoped that Marolyn wouldn't do anything to spoil Victoria's fun that night.

The Island Resort was a happy place despite the troubles they'd had. There was something about a tropical island that lifted a person's spirit. Maybe it was the sunshine—all that vitamin D boosting the immune system and the healthy glow it painted on winter skin. Or maybe it was the positive ions given off by the sea water, sucked into thirsty lungs—all that invigorating energy coursing through the blood.

Solly thought it was the good food and slower tempo of island life that made the guests feel happy. Harriet thought it had more to do with leaving the pressures of their lives behind for a completely different environment; one where, for a short while at least, they could feel carefree and relaxed. No worries. No troubles. No anxiety.

It was the same for most of the staff. They had access to the same vitamin D, positive ions, and good food. They had beautiful, airy living quarters and working conditions that were some of the best on the planet. Since opening seven months before, employee turnover (other than a few who had to be let go) was zero.

Despite the murders of several guests and a co-worker,

Harriet loved her job as public relations director for the resort. Every time she turned around, she found some new feature to highlight in her ads. One constant she focused on was the resort's efforts to meet every guest's needs.

Besides the wedding, the resort would host the originally scheduled family reunion party with music, a dance floor, hors d'oeuvres, and drinks. The guests' meals were included in the weekly resort fee, but the food and drink for the wedding and reunion party were extra and needed to be itemized, a task that fell on her shoulders. She sent up a quick prayer that the wedding would go off without a hitch.

Scanning through her lists to see what still needed to be checked off, she realized she hadn't spoken to the resort's chef after Marolyn's last menu change.

Harriet had discovered early on that the best way to work with Chef was to simply tell him what she needed and then leave him alone, which suited them both just fine. Chef's food was always a notch above superb and a major draw for the resort. She had featured his food in several ad campaigns, although the chef himself refused to be videoed.

"My food speaks for me. You don't want my damned face in your ads," Chef grumbled. She had tried to talk him into doing an ad focused on his standing as one of the world's few five-star chefs, but he flatly refused. "I don't want my ugly puss plastered all over the ass end of a bus."

Harriet suspected that Chef's gruff exterior hid a shy reserve, so she hadn't pushed, even though she could have told him she never ran ads on buses—their ass ends or their sides. Bus ads did not appeal to their upscale demographic.

She was about to cut the call when Chef answered. Chef Lebrecque, a tall, portly figure with silvered, dark hair worn slicked back into a ponytail and a loud baritone that filled the room from one end of the kitchens to the other, ruled his domain with an iron fist. She would be shocked if he said he needed help, but she felt obliged to ask.

"Chef. I'm calling to see if there are any last minute items you need help with for the reunion party and wedding."

He narrowed his shrewd, dark brown eyes at Harriet. "If the Packard woman has changed her mind again, it is too late. The food is mostly prepared."

"She tried yesterday," Harriet admitted, "but I told her it was too late to get in three hundred baby octopi." She couldn't help herself; she grinned at the expression on Chef's face.

"Baby–" Chef spluttered a few choice swear words. "The woman is insane."

"That seems to be the general consensus. So you're all set? I'm checking last-minute items off my lists."

"The food is set. No more changes."

"Agreed. Thank you, Chef." Harriet ended the call.

It would be a miracle if no one took out the mother of the bride before the week was up.

Ghost Ship

Bolkarus Station

Omega Lab

Mars Base

Junkyard Dog Collection Books 1-3

Junkyard Dog Collection 2 Books 4-6

Junkyard Dog Collection 3 Books 7-9

Junkyard Dog Collection 4 Books 10-13

Junkyard Dog Omnibus

Steampunk Heart

UPHEAVAL SERIES

Slow Walk

Edge of Reality

Solstice Moon

Upheaval Series Collection

MYSTERY

Gypsy Gold

Dark Horse

Desert Star

ABOUT THE AUTHOR

Charley Marsh's curiosity drove her to climb mountains, canoe rivers, and explore caves and wilderness areas from Maine to California. She's been shot at, caught in a desert flash flood, and almost drowned off the Maine coast. Once she tobogganed down a 5,000+ foot mountain.

Life is always an adventure if you have the right attitude.

Charley never set out to be a storyteller, but looking back on the elaborate lies she made up as a troubled teen she can see that she always had the makings. Now, in the words of Lawrence Block, she happily "makes up lies for fun and profit."